MURDER IN MENORCA

CAT PRESTON

CAT PRESTON

Copyright © 2015 Cat Preston

ISBN-13: 978-1522906988

ICBN-10: 1522906983

All rights reserved.

MURDER IN MENORCA

CHAPTER ONE

"We've been here for 3 days and it's as if you've been staying here for months Mum!" Will, Abby's son, laughed.

Abby Tennant and her two sons, Luke and William, were sitting by the pool at their hotel in Arenal D'En Castell, Menorca, enjoying the 30 degree heat and free watermelon slices the barman was handing out. William's comment was aimed at the fact that during the last 20 minutes of sitting on their sunbeds more than 6 different guests had approached Abby for a chat.

True, Abby thought, she was a chatterbox, but she didn't see anything wrong with that surely? At least, nobody here seemed to mind, and where was the fun in going on holiday and not befriending the other guests?

"Hello Abby, lovely day hey!?" Case in point Abby thought as she smiled as Eveline Dawson and Jane Fox wandered by. Abby had met them on the day they arrived and had warmed to them instantly. Both women were the best of friends, and had apparently been so for over 60 years, having met when their parents lived in the same village.

"We still on for cocktails later?" Jane called out as they went.

"Of course" Abby smiled.

"You know them two are old enough to be our grandparents don't you Mum?" Will asked.

"And?" Abby shrugged, "Did you know Eveline was one of the first women to climb Everest, and Jane spent a year volunteering in Borneo helping orphaned orangutans? They're cool! And their stories are amazing."

"That is cool!" Luke conceded.

Of course, nothing Abby said would be cool to Will, being a 15 year old boy Abby reckoned nothing she said or did could ever be thought of as cool by her Doctor Who-obsessed nerdy son. Luke on the other hand, now being 18 and off to University in September, had suddenly blossomed into a lovely young man. Gone were the sullen moods and the rolling eyes every time his Mum said something, replaced with a much more adult outlook. Abby marvelled at the change, proud and a tad confused all at the same time.

"Who's up for an ice-cream?" she asked, knowing that as old as they were getting, they would still jump at the chance of a chocolate ice-cream cone.

After ice creams, Abby and the boys went back to the room and showered before setting off for the evening; Abby was headed for cocktails with Eveline and Jane, while Luke and Will were headed down to the beach to meet up with the other holiday kids.

Abby had been looking forward to the gossip, and listening to some more of their wild stories. Neither woman had married, and instead had filled their lives with adventure, visiting places Abby had only read about in novels or seen on David Attenborough shows. Part of her wished she'd led a more interesting life, but then she knew if she had she wouldn't have her boys, or the special relationship they shared, which was worth the world to Abby, especially after the bitter break down of her marriage, which still stung even 10 years later.

She'd found the ladies by the poolside bar, laughing loudly. "Ladies," she smiled.

"Abby! We were just talking about you!" they grinned back. "You should come with us tomorrow," they suggested.

"Why, where are you going?" Abby asked.

"We're going on a bit of a cultural trip. We're going to do a whistlestop tour of the island and then spend a night in Mahon." Eveline explained.

"Ooh, sounds lovely!" Abby enthused.

"Yes, but the getting up at the crack of dawn part of the trip sounds anything but," Jane grumbled.

"Oh shush, woman!" Eveline retorted. "4am is hardly the crack of dawn, in fact I'm pretty sure it's much earlier than that!" laughed Eveline.

"Ouch! Yeah, I think I'll give that one a miss thank you very much!" Abby decided. She wasn't one for early mornings, much preferring to snuggle up under the duvet until it was absolutely necessary to get up. 7am was early enough for Abby, particularly when on holiday.

"Agnes!" Eveline shouted, breaking Abby out of her thoughts. Abby looked over in the direction that Eveline was waving, and saw an older lady hobbling over to their table.

"Are you okay dear?" Eveline asked as the lady got closer. The lady's face was pale, made even paler by her purple-pink hair, forming a shock of tight curls on her head. "Agnes?"

Agnes finally looked up, seemingly only just recognising the ladies as she made to pass by the table. "I'm sorry," she stammered. "I'm in a bit of a hurry. Can I catch you ladies later?" she asked hurriedly.

"Sure. Is everything okay?" Jane asked.

"Hmm??" Agnes looked up, confused. "Oh, erm, yes, yes of course," she stammered before continuing to move through the tables.

"That was strange," Eveline commented. "She's usually so chatty."

"Mmm," Jane agreed, nodding her head. "She's been coming here for 6 years you know?"

"Really?" Abby looked over her shoulder at the receding figure of Mrs Cook, hunched over and uncertain on her feet. "She doesn't look very well."

"Oh she isn't dear." Eveline confirmed. "She's on god knows how many different types of medication. She has heart problems I think. I don't even think she was cleared to come on this holiday from what she was telling me."

"Yes but when you know it's your time you don't want to be stuck in some nursing home, do you!?" Jane argued. And Abby had to agree. She would much rather be enjoying her last days on earth relaxing in a bar than spending it cooped up in a nursing home.

After cocktails and dinner, Abby hugged the women goodbye, wishing them a fantastic trip, before heading back to her room to grab her tablet.

CHAPTER TWO

Abby had spent the morning walking in the nature reserve and wanted to check out her photographs on a bigger screen and use her favourite app to adjust some of the colours. The hotel didn't have free wifi so she had already become a regular at the restaurant opposite, taking advantage of their free wifi to check her emails and catch up on the news.

"Hola Abby!" Paolo called out from across the restaurant as Abby walked through the main door.

"Hola Paulo!" Abby returned, practicing her rusty Spanish. She barely remembered anything from school, though "Tengo trefe anos" had always stuck in her head.

Abby grabbed a table close to the juke box with comfy leather chairs and set her tablet on the table as Paulo walked over. "Café con leche?" he asked, already familiar with her regular evening order.

"Por favor" Abby smiled.

As Paolo went back to the bar and busied himself with creating her favourite drink Abby opened up her tablet and logged on to the Wifi.

As she waited for the tablet to connect to the wifi she looked up and scanned the room, looking for any familiar faces. The restaurant was fairly quiet but her attention was drawn to a sleeping lady in the far corner of the room. She chuckled to herself as she realised it was Mrs Cook from earlier.

Abby wondered what the old lady must have been doing in the few hours since she'd last seen her, it must have been something good given how exhausted she now obviously was.

When Paolo came over with her coffee Abby motioned over to Mrs Cook, "Has she been here long?" she asked.

"I don't know," Paulo confessed. "I've not long been here myself, but I know she's been here longer than me." He shrugged. "Do you think I should go and wake her?"

"No," Abby suggested. "I'd just let her sleep. She looked pretty stressed earlier today. I'd leave her to nap. If she doesn't wake by the time I'm ready to leave I'll give her a nudge."

"Okay. Gracias." And off he went, his attention already drawn to another customer.

Abby loved it here. The restaurant was a relaxed affair, serving also as a café and regular haunt for the ex-pats dotted around the resort. She had decided she would make this place her regular coffee haunt on day one of arriving at the resort, and had been here every day of her holiday so far, with no intention of missing a day – the coffee was just too good!

After uploading her photos to her new Instagram account, and getting a bit too excited over the fact that she now had one new follower, Abby closed the case to her tablet and sat back, relaxing in her chair and wondering for the first time this evening what her boys were up to.

This would probably be the last time she'd have them both together like this, with Luke going away to University next month and Will not wanting to travel alone with his Mum anymore. She'd already had to bribe them to come away this year, promising Luke some help with expenses for his University digs if he would come, as Will had categorically refused to go without him.

Abby knew it was better to have such brotherly love than for them to be constantly bickering and she was worried about how much Will would miss his older brother when he was away. Will had already started talking about going up to Liverpool to visit him in his new digs. Something Abby was already stressing about, having come from Liverpool and knowing how much of a draw it was to young people. You didn't have anything like the night life down on the coast, in Kent, where they now lived.

"Another coffee, Abby?" Paulo interrupted Abby's thoughts, and she shook her head from side to side, filing away her thoughts for another time.

"No thank you, Paolo. I better head off." Abby stood to leave, pulling a few coins out of the pocket of her grey linen trousers and stacking them on the table.

"Abby...." Paulo motioned over to the table where Mrs Cook still sat, her head rolled over to one side.

Wow, that must be uncomfortable, Abby thought as she acknowledged Paulo's request and made her way over to Mrs Cook's table. As she got closer to the table though something didn't feel right. Mrs Cook's head looked a little bit more than uncomfortable and her arms were fully extended, drooping beside her body, her hands lifeless and bony-looking.

Abby approached carefully, tapping Mrs Cook on the shoulder. Her shoulder seemed cold to the touch and Abby snatched her hand away, a feeling of unease passing over her.

"Mrs Cook..." Abby shook Mrs Cook's shoulder now, and getting nowhere turned to Paulo and shouted, "Call an ambulance!"

Crap! Abby thought. How long has she been sitting here? And I just left her? Guilt swept over her and she felt her legs start to give way.

Paulo rushed over. "What is it?" he asked. He pushed Mrs Cook's head back so he could check her pulse and then jumped back as Mrs Cook looked out at them, lifeless, her eyes glazed and empty looking.

CAT PRESTON

CHAPTER THREE

"Oh my god!" Abby exclaimed, her hand hovering over her mouth, stopping a scream from coming out. Paolo pulled a chair out just as Abby's legs collapsed from under her. She plonked down into it, her head falling into her hands, barely able to stop the tears that threatened to spill out.

"What can we..." Abby started, but Paolo had already run over to the phone, grasping it in his hands and redialling the ambulance. He muttered something in Spanish and then came back over and checked Mrs Cook's pulse. What must have been seconds felt like an eternity as Abby watched the poor woman's body, cursing herself for not checking on her earlier.

"She's dead, Abby" Paolo confirmed. "They're sending an ambulance and the police over right now. They should be here in minutes. Do you want me to get you anything?" he asked, the consummate host.

"No.." Abby managed. What would she have?! God, she'd been sitting here drinking coffee while Mrs Cook had been slowly dying for all she knew.

Abby stared into the wall, unable to move, unable to process the feelings that were whirling around in her head. She must have sat there for a good few minutes as next thing she knew someone was placing their hand gently on her arm, asking her if she was alright.

Abby looked up, noticing the uniform first. The green medics uniform, attached to a kind face with eyes full of concern.

"What happened?" she asked.

"We'd usually be the ones asking you that," an English voice observed. Abby looked behind the paramedic to see a tall, dark-haired man, watching her inquisitively. As he moved closer and extended his hand, Abby noticed the scruffy 5 o'clock shadow on his face.

"Detective James McEwan" the man introduced himself.

Abby nodded, though she had no idea what she was nodding at. "Sorry, I'm just....I just...." She didn't know what to say. "She was sitting here, and I was over there drinking coffee thinking she was just napping. I didn't know." Abby tried to explain.

"Okay," said Detective McEwan, "Let's start from the top. Can you run through your evening for me starting just before you came in here so I can get a timeline down."

Abby shifted uncomfortably in her seat, anxious to now get back to her boys. "My boys..." she muttered.

"I'm sorry Mrs...., I'm sorry can I take your name first?" Detective McEwan asked.

Abby ran her fingers through her hair, not realising how flustered she looked. James could see the fear in her eyes and knew he needed to reassure her before she went into shock. He motioned one of the police officers over and asked them to bring over some water.

"Take a sip Mrs...., it'll make you feel better" James handed Abby a glass of water and she took it gladly, gulping it down.

The water seemed to do the trick, and Abby asked whether she could have another glass.

Having downed the second glass of water Abby felt much better and tried to concentrate on the man sitting opposite her, waiting patiently for her answer.

"Yes, sorry, it's Miss Tennant."

"Miss Tennant," James repeated, writing her name down in his notepad. "And your boys, where are they?"

"Oh who knows!" Abby breathed out, "Probably down at the beach with their friends. They're teenagers, it's just, you know, this happens and all you want to do is check your own are okay." Abby knotted her fingers together, twisting her hands in her lap, trying to concentrate on calming herself.

"I'm sorry," she apologised again, "I must look a complete mess. It's just a bit of a shock that's all. You don't expect to find someone, well I've never seen anyone, you know, dead, before."

Abby ran her hands over her face. She felt like an idiot, she couldn't string a sentence together, and couldn't stop fidgeting.

"Can I go to the loo?" she asked. Maybe if she splashed some water on her face she could get her thoughts together and turn into a somewhat more cohesive woman.

James let her go, hoping she'd come back feeling a little better. At this rate he'd still be interviewing her at breakfast time.

Five minutes later Abby breezed in. "Okay, I'm feeling a bit better now. Sorry, that just floored me, I mean it's not every day you find someone you kind of know dead is it?" Abby confided as she sat down in her seat again. The water-on-face trick had worked wonders and she felt much more with it, ready to be questioned and to get back to her room.

And questioned she was. James took her through her evening in minute detail, from finishing up her dinner to the moment he arrived. She told him as much as she could remember and tried not to embellish on any of the details or speculate as to what happened. She also admitted to feeling guilty about leaving Mrs Cook for so long, and wondered whether she could have saved her but James assured her that Mrs Cook had been dead for a little while so 30 minutes wouldn't have made a bit of a difference.

One of the police officers came over and quietly whispered something in James's ear. Abby found herself craning her neck to try to get closer to hear, then chastised herself for being so disrespectful. She caught James's eye and noticed he was looking past her and into the room, and as she turned to see what he was looking at the ambulance men walked past her carrying Mrs Cook on a stretcher.

"Oh!" Abby jumped as Mrs Cook's arm flopped out of the blanket. She pushed her chair back and stood, trying to back away from the body, but as she did so her foot twisted and she tripped, landing on the arm of James's chair, almost sitting on his arm.

"Oh god, I'm sorry!" she squealed. James stood, and grabbed Abby's upper arms and gently moved her to the side so the ambulance men could continue past the table and into the waiting ambulance.

"You're very jumpy!" he commented, trying not to find the humour in the situation as she was still trying to back away.

"Sorry, god, I'm just a mess!"

"Look, I think I've got everything I need here, how about I walk you back to your room and if I need any more information I'll know where to find you?" James suggested.

"Oh yes, please. I think I just want to get out of here now!" Abby confessed.

James spoke to one of the officers for a minute before turning back toward Abby and motioning her, "Come on then Miss Tennant, let's get you back to your room!"

She smiled, thankfully. "Phew!" she murmured.

James smiled at her as he made for the door, holding it open as Abby walked through. As it closed behind them Abby grabbed James's arm, about to link it before she realised what she was doing. She jumped away from him, "god, sorry, I don't know what I'm doing" she smiled at him ruefully.

"It's okay Miss Tennant, you've had a rough night."

"Please, call me Abby" Abby interrupted him, "Miss Tennant just sounds strange..." Inside Abby was screaming at herself to shut up, what must this man think of her, she was a bumbling mess. Not at all how she liked to project herself usually. Abby prided herself on being a strong and independent working mother, and was mortified at how she was acting. "Look, I'm sorry, I was divorced not long ago, Tennant still feels a bit weird, but then nothing about this isn't weird so..." her voice drifted off as she caught James's expression.

He was looking at her in a way she'd never been looked at before, or was she just imagining it. Maybe, but wow, those eyes, she could definitely lose herself in those eyes, she thought.

James linked her arm companionably and began walking. "Stop apologising," he chastised her gently, "You've nothing to be apologising for".

They walked in silence across the road and up the path towards the hotel. Abby led the way to her room and as they approached it found herself slowing considerably, not yet ready to go in.

"This is me," she said, regrettably, unable to stop their approach. She turned towards him, ready to thank him for walking her back, but the words stuck in her throat as her eyes fell on his lips, his tongue darting out and licking his bottom lip. She dragged her eyes up to his and found herself gazing into them. He was watching her expression intently, as if looking for some kind of clue. Their bodies were still close and her arm was still entwined in his.

"Mum!"

Abby dragged her attention away from the beckoning gaze of the handsome detective and towards the direction of the shouting voices. "Mum!" it came again.

She caught sight of her youngest then, William, running across the gardens towards their apartment.

James stepped back, putting some distance between them and taking on a more professional stance. Abby looked back at those eyes of his but whatever moment she'd imagined had gone, and James stood, looking out towards Will as he came crashing to a halt barely inches in front of James. To give him his due, James didn't flinch at all. Abby did. She had a horrible feeling Will was going to hurtle right into James, he'd been running that fast.

"Luke is still down by the beach, he sent me back for some money. Do you have any?" Will asked excitedly.

Abby was torn between sticking her hand in her pocket and pulling out a random note, to instructing her sons to come back in instantly, after all, she could do with not being alone right now. And just as she tried to formulate words...

"Hi," James extended his hand towards Will, "I'm Detective McEwan. Your mum has just been witness to a death so if you could grab your brother and come back to the apartment, I think she probably needs company tonight." He explained as gently as he could.

"What!?" Will exclaimed, open-mouthed. "Really, Mum? Are you okay?"

Abby could do little but smile. She suddenly felt all emotional seeing the concern rush across her son's face. She wanted to give him a hug, a never-ending one, but knew she'd just embarrass him so held back.

Will wasn't so reserved. He bear hugged his Mum before racing for the beach to get his older brother, Luke.

"I'll stay with you, come on, let's get in and get that kettle on." James ordered. It was just what Abby needed, something mundane to do amidst the mess she had walked into tonight. James sat on the stool at the breakfast nook in the kitchenette and watched her intently as she busied herself dragging cups out of the cupboard and preparing them for tea. She grabbed a packet of chocolate biscuits from the same cupboard as she heard James gently chuckle behind her.

"What?" she questioned as she turned to look at him.

"Nothing, just...you're prepared aren't you!?" he chuckled again.

"What, the biscuits? Are you joking me? If I didn't have biscuits for dunking the boys would sulk for days." Abby smiled, and then caught herself smiling and felt guilty about it.

"Don't do that," James scolded lightly, seemingly knowing her thought process. "Just because someone died today doesn't mean you can't have a laugh and a joke. It's how you get through things. And it's entirely natural." He stood then, took a step towards her, desperate to brush the errant hair from her face, just as Will and Luke came bursting through the apartment door.

"Mum, are you okay?" Luke asked, worry etched in his voice. The bear hugging resumed and Abby relaxed against the weight of her eldest son as he guided her over to the couch and put the tea and biscuits in front of her.

James stood on the edge, watching as Abby's son flitted around her, making sure she was okay. He made his move to leave and promised to come back the next day and update Abby on what had happened, and check she had recovered.

Abby nodded, and smiled her thanks as Luke pulled a blanket in from the bedroom and draped it over his Mum.

"What are you doing?" Abby laughed.

"This is what you always do for me when I'm not well. Couch, blanket, biscuits, movie...right?"

Abby laughed, "Not when it's 20 plus degrees outside!"

James closed the door gently, stepping quietly away from the house as the sound of laughter filled the air. He stood for a few seconds, his head spinning, trying to get the image of Abby Tennant out of his brain. Why did he suddenly feel like turning round and knocking and being asked to be let back in?

MURDER IN MENORCA

CHAPTER FOUR

Abby and the boys were stopped more than 20 times as they made their way down for breakfast, or so it felt. Everyone had heard about what had happened last night, Abby wouldn't have been surprised if there was a poster announcement of Mrs Cook's death up at the front desk, the circumstances apparently being that well-known.

Given that Abby was the one who found Mrs Cook everyone wanted to make a beeline in her direction, asking what had happened and how she'd known she was dead. It was morbid, but then people were when it came to death Abby guessed.

Alongside everyone's curiosity, it also seemed that everyone had their very own story to tell of Mrs Cook, and they also all wanted to share their story with Abby. Before finishing breakfast, Abby had counted 30 people who had approached their table on the pretence of asking how she was. Some were sincere, shocked at how she must have felt and sympathetic, but others just wanted to find out the grizzly details. There were even some who contemplated whether the death was natural or not, and intimated to hushed conversations they had seen or worried glances and careful behaviour they had noticed that only now seemed relevant.

The boys were fascinated by the whole charade, and were, like any teenage boys, immensely enjoying their new-found fame amongst the young women who kept throwing furtive glances and giggling behind closed hands. Abby took it all in her stride, confident it would all blow over once everyone realised that poor Mrs Cook had simply died of a heart attack or something else completely natural. 'Surely that was all there could be to it?' she pondered as she tucked into her fourth pastry of the day, her own curiosity being piqued ever so slightly.

After breakfast Abby decided to head out for a walk to clear her head, and mostly to get away from all the busybodies. She was sick of being asked about the events of the previous night and just wanted some space to process everything in her own mind before people continued with their theories and assumptions.

She took the road to the beach and wandered down the boardwalk that looked like it had recently been put in. The walk took her over to the nature park and as she ambled amongst the tall trees she relived the events of the previous evening in her head, mentally taking herself through everything she had seen and trying to work out if she'd missed anything out. The thought that Mrs Cook's death could be anything but natural had Abby thinking about whether she'd missed a vital clue or had inadvertently dismissed something that otherwise could have stood out.

Abby remembered Mrs Cook being at the restaurant when she arrived but couldn't remember whether she had been asleep the whole time or not. Maybe she'd been awake? Maybe she'd been struggling to breathe?

She knew Mrs Cook had had a heart problem from talking with Eveline and Jane, and also knew she took pills for her heart, so maybe she'd missed taking them, or took one too many? But that didn't make sense. Maybe she'd been upset by whoever she'd been talking to on the phone, as reported by Ernie O'Brien over breakfast this morning. Or maybe Jerry Hartwell had been right and Mrs Cook had had enough of her bickering family and had taken enough sleeping pills to kill an elephant. Hmmm, maybe this Jerry Hartwell guy wasn't a very reliable witness, thought Abby, giggling to herself.

What did she really know? She knew Mrs Cook had died last night. She knew she'd seemed out of sorts when she had seen her in the hotel just yesterday. She must have had a lot on her mind as she'd seemed distracted, but by what? And did that have anything to do with her death? Abby concluded that before spending any more time thinking about what could and couldn't have happened, she really needed to know if Mrs Cook had passed naturally or whether there was foul play involved. The only way to do that was to head back to the hotel and see whether anyone had any more recent information.

Resolved on her course of action, Abby headed back, and no sooner had she walked through the hotel lobby than she came face to face with Detective McEwan.

"Hi," she greeted him warmly.

James nodded his head curtly. He had been caught off guard by his emotions last night and he'd decided the only way to deal with them was to pack them down and throw sand over them. He couldn't get involved with the main witness of a case, and what would be the point even if he did? He'd only have to say goodbye at the end of her holiday and then what, pine away the rest of his days? No, that wouldn't do. Instead, he'd decided to play the cool cop and distance himself straightaway.

Abby chose not to notice his coldness though, and smiled on through his frosty reception. 'What a smile!' he thought, before mentally smacking himself.

"I have just a few more questions if I may?" James motioned towards a table in the lobby.

Abby followed his lead and sat gingerly, waiting to hear what James had to say.

"Did you notice anyone hovering by Mrs Cook at all throughout the evening?" James asked, getting right to the gist of his questioning. He may not be being very professional, diving straight in with the difficult questions, but he didn't feel like wasting time.

"No," Abby confirmed, a hint of indecision in her voice.

"And you're sure about that? There was no-one by the witness when you entered the restaurant, or at any time while you were there?" James persisted.

"Not that I can remember. Why do you ask?"

"Just routine questions, Miss Tennant. Did you happen to notice whether Mrs Cook was awake or supposedly asleep when you entered the restaurant?" James continued.

"No. I was just thinking about that before, but I don't recall noticing her awake at any point." Abby confirmed. "Is that an important point?" she asked, suspicion edging into her voice.

"Just routine again."

"What's going on?" Abby asked, getting agitated by James's bluntness. "Have I done something wrong?"

"I'm just following routine Miss Tennant" James scolded.

Abby stared right through into his soul, or so it felt. Her eyes bore down on him with such an intensity that he wanted to take a step back, to increase the distance between them. He pushed the chair he was perched on away from the table and stood, seemingly done with his questioning. Abby had other ideas though.

She jumped up and grabbed his arm. "Detective McEwan," she said sternly.

He turned, his hand reaching for hers and removing it from his arm, where the imprint burnt intto his skin. "I'm rather busy if you don't mind..." he started but Abby's feistiness won out.

"What have I done?" she demanded. "You couldn't have been nicer last night, and yet now, look at you, treating me like a criminal or something. I demand to know what I've done!" she pouted.

James sighed, annoyed with himself at being led so astray by his petty emotions. "I'm sorry," he said, dragging his fingers through his hair. "I'm just tired. Sorry, I shouldn't be taking it out on you."

"No, you shouldn't" Abby acknowledged, but with a softness to her voice she hadn't had before. She stared at him, trying to weigh him up and decide on her next course of action, before finally asking, "Do you want a coffee?". He looked tired, and it couldn't be easy doing this job, she thought, suddenly concerned, and wanting to be nice to him after he had been so considerate the previous evening.

"No, I best not. I have to get back to the office and report in. It's not been the best of days so far. Raincheck?" he managed a smile, cringing inside at how ridiculous he was being. Professionalism, man, he wanted to scream at himself.

"I was thinking about Mrs Cook," Abby started. "I forgot to say last night, I'd seen her earlier in the day and she'd seemed very distracted. I just, I don't know if that is relevant at all but I thought it might be. Some guests have been saying she had some family problems, I don't know whether that could have caused her stress or contributed in some way…" she trailed off, unsure what she was trying to convey exactly.

"Thanks" James said. "But you can't go around asking questions of guests, that's my job, not yours."

"I wasn't!" Abby retorted, "I had people coming up to me all morning speculating about what happened to poor Mrs Cook, I'm just relaying what's been said." Abby was starting to get annoyed again, and wanted nothing more than to walk away before she said something she'd regret.

"Well if anyone says anything else, just point them in my direction, okay?" James shot back.

"Fine. Look, if that's all the questions you had then I need to go." She could barely contain her anger towards him, and if he hadn't been a police officer may have already lost her temper.

He dismissed her with a nod and she jumped up from the table and stalked away, muttering insults under her breath. What the hell was his problem!? Abby wondered. What had she done to deserve that!? Okay he may be tired, but that was no excuse for being rude!

Seething, Abby headed to her room just long enough to change into her swimming costume and then headed down to the pool to swim away her annoyance at a man that only hours earlier had been high on her list of likeable males. Bloody men! she fumed, pounding at the water with every stroke.

CAT PRESTON

CHAPTER FIVE

Feeling much better, and calmer, only an hour later after swimming a few lengths and chilling in a sunbed for a while, Abby decided not to let James ruin her day, and get on with it. She texted her sons to make sure they were okay and then headed over to the restaurant for an early lunch. Swimming made her so hungry!

Paolo greeted Abby like an old friend, settling her down in the comfiest chair and bringing over a delicious coffee with a biscotti as a pre-dinner treat. By the time Abby had wolfed down a steak baguette and chips she felt like a new woman, invigorated and ready for action. She dared James to confront her now, she thought, a smile breaking out on her sun-kissed face.

Paolo headed over with another coffee and Abby asked if anything else had happened since last night. Sitting down in the chair opposite hers, Paolo looked about him conspiratorially then leaned in close to Abby, his voice barely above a whisper. "They question me for a long time," Paolo confided. "But that is not the worse. They take Gino in to the police station."

Abby gasped, "What did he do!?" she questioned.

"Gino's a good boy, he's done nothing. But he wasn't always a good boy. He has a past, a history with the local police, but he was doing well and keeping out of trouble you know." aolo sighed, and Abby looked at him anew, noticing his drawn face, the bags under his eyes and stubble longer than usual.

"Paulo, have you slept at all since last night?" Abby asked, concerned for her new friend.

"I am far too worried to sleeping. I am worried for Gino. What will I tell his mother? I promised her he would be a okay." Paolo's head dropped into his hands as his shoulders sank down into his body.

"Did Gino have anything to do with Mrs Cook's death?" Abby asked gently, her hand reaching out and patting Paolo's.

"No!" Paolo said emphatically. "Of course not! He's really a very good boy now. He's not been in trouble for a long time."

"Ok." Abby comforted. "Then the police will realise this and will let him go shortly, I am sure."

"How can you be so sure?" Paolo challenged. "They hate him there. They will just look for an excuse to lock him away. The chief dislikes him greatly after Gino got his daughter into trouble."

"The local police maybe, but it's not just the local police who are investigating this death. Detective McEwan wouldn't let an innocent man be charged for anything he didn't do, I am sure of it."

Paolo wasn't convinced, and it took Abby a lot more convincing Paolo of James's moral standing to persuade him that the truth would prevail and Gino would be set free. Abby may not know James very well, or indeed at all really, but she was confident in her ability to read people, and for as much as he had annoyed her that morning, he didn't come across as someone who would skirt around the truth.

As she thought more about James, and Gino and the fact that he had been taken in for questioning, she realised that this apparent natural death may be anything but. She was no policeman, not even remotely involved with the law at all, but she'd seen her fair share of detective series and cop shows and she didn't think people were arrested and taken away for questioning when a little old lady had died of natural causes.

No, something else must be up. Maybe Ernie O'Brien was onto something, and Mrs Cook's death was caused by someone else. Was Mrs Cook murdered?! Abby tried processing that thought, as she re-assessed all she knew about the woman.

Sure, she was cantankerous, but given her age Abby thought she had every right to be. What if she'd done what Jerry Hartwell had suggested and spiked her own drink? Would that lead to someone's arrest? Could someone hate an old lady so much they couldn't just wait for natural causes to take their course? Maybe there was a reason Mrs Cook had to die now? But on holiday? Who would know her well enough on holiday? None of it made any sense.

Obviously, James would know the truth, but she couldn't ask him. Maybe last night he would have shared, but not after his behaviour this morning. She'd done something to irritate him, she was sure of that, but what that something was she had no idea. Maybe it was her reaction to the body? Did she overreact when confronted with death? Surely he couldn't hold that against her? It's not every day you find a dead person sitting in a chair not far across from you. Surely she was allowed to freak out!? Surely other people had freaked out even more!? No, that couldn't be it, and if it was then he was an even bigger idiot than she had given him credit for.

She hadn't got the impression that he was an idiot though, not from her first meeting with him. He'd come across as really nice, and genuinely concerned for her well-being. Had she reacted so badly to Mrs Cook's death that her whole emotional system had turned off? Abby prided herself on being a good judge of character, and usually hit the nail on the head with first impressions. Her instincts couldn't have gone that wrong!

"Right!" Abby said out loud, startling Paolo out of his reverie. "I'm going to talk to Detective McEwan and get to the bottom of all this," she decided, standing up and almost knocking over her empty coffee cup as she did.

CAT PRESTON

CHAPTER SIX

"Talk to me about what?" a voice asked from behind.

Abby slowly turned, her embarrassment flooding her cheeks red. James stood almost directly behind her – why hadn't she even heard him coming? – looking at her with a half-amused half-annoyed look on his face, as though he hadn't yet decided how to react to her. Abby pulled herself up tall, her back straight, her shoulders down, trying to fill herself with a confidence she was yet to feel.

"I was just coming to find you!" she stammered, annoyed at the hesitation in her voice.

"Why?" James asked, and Abby got the intense feeling that she was being mocked. A flicker of irritation ran across her face, which made James's sultry smile spread even wider.

"Why do I get the feeling that you're toying with me?" Abby blurted out, wishing instantly that she'd kept her mouth shut.

James barely supressed a laugh as he revelled in her obvious discomfort, but then he saw the flash of hurt deep in her eyes and regretted being the brash bully he was portraying.

"Sorry," he laughed, "you're just so damn cute!" and then couldn't help but smile at her. There he'd said it, she was cute. And she bloody was, James thought. Cute, beautiful, engaging.

"Cute!?!" Abby shouted. "Cute!?" her hands moved to her hips as her stance took on a more aggressive demeanour, her eyes glaring at him now. "I am not cute!" she exclaimed, "Cute is for toddlers and tiny little girls with bunches in their hair! Cute!" she guffawed. "You have some bloody nerve!" she followed up.

Paolo had made a swift retreat behind the bar at the first sign of Detective McEwan, and was now nowhere to be seen. James took a quick look around the bar, and seeing no one else there stepped closer to a now steaming Abby.

"I didn't mean cute," he tried. "Well, now that's a lie. I do find you cute." He was now standing right in front of Abby, she could see his chest heaving up and down, feel his warm breath on her cheeks. He gently touched her upper arm with his fingers.

"I hate that word," Abby stuttered, suddenly finding it very hard to concentrate on anything but how a couple of hairs were trying to escape out of James's crisp, white shirt. She sucked in her bottom lip, her eyes locking in on his as they watched her.

"Coffee?" Paolo broke the tension that simmered in the air and James stepped back, still looking intently into Abby's eyes.

Paolo laid the tray on the table with 2 mugs of coffee then made off back into the kitchen, unsure whether he should be staying or going. It certainly didn't look like Abby needed any help, Detective McEwan maybe did, Paolo thought as he scarpered.

Abby broke the eye contact and sat back down into her chair.

"Do you want to explain what the hell is going on here?" she demanded, breathing heavily. "This morning you almost bit my head off, and now, now, this, whatever this is!" she exclaimed hotly.

James sunk into the chair across from Abby. How the heck should he know what was going on!? He was an emotional wreck. What was this woman doing to him?

"I think it's pretty evident that I find you extremely attractive," he explained, his voice husky and even. He sighed deeply, "I find myself constantly apologising to you for something or other. I think I've apologised to you more than I ever did to my ex-wife," he joked. "My professionalism has apparently abandoned me and I find myself behaving like a naughty school boy around you." He glanced at her as he tried to explain his erratic behaviour. "Maybe we should talk about whatever it is you wanted to talk with me about?" James suggested, feeling more than a little embarrassed and desperately wanting to change the conversation.

"I can't even remember!" Abby confessed. Besides, she wanted to continue the conversation they were having right now. She wanted an explanation for James's brash treatment of her this morning, and apparently finding her attractive simply wasn't going to cut it. Did he honestly think she was born yesterday? Surely he didn't think she'd fall for the blatant flattery angle, trying to deviate away from his true feelings? Extremely attractive indeed, she thought, I wonder how many times he's tried that one on other women.

"I remember," she almost shouted triumphantly. "Gino!" And all of a sudden the guarded mask came down over his face.

"Ha!" Abby followed up. "Now I want to talk about something and you decide now would be the best time to shut right down, is that it? I'm not falling for your hunky man in a tizz act, Detective McEwan. Now, can you tell me why Gino has been arrested, and none of your nonsense either!" she scolded, indignantly.

James stared at her. A hunky man act?? Was this woman for real!? He struggled to find something to say and wondered why he desperately wanted to make her believe he wasn't trying to pull some kind of act over her, wow, what kind of men was this women used to!?

"Gino has connections with the local police." James plucked for honesty. "They are simply following procedure," James explained.

"You mean they've gone for the first obvious connection?" Abby retorted.

"Look Abby, I shouldn't be telling you this, Jesus I shouldn't be talking to you at all, but Gino was the only one here when Mrs Cook arrived at the restaurant. Gino was the one who served Mrs Cook, and Gino was the one who had conveniently disappeared when Mrs Cook was found dead. It's standard procedure that we would follow up on all that, surely you understand that?" James implored. It was important to him that Abby was on his side, he couldn't fathom out why but he didn't want her harbouring bad feelings toward him, even if she did think he was playing some kind of act.

"So I assume from all this new action that Mrs Cook didn't die of natural causes then?" Abby asked.

"You assume right." James conceded.

Abby sat back in her chair and cast her eyes over James.

"And you can stop looking at me like that!" James warned.

"Like what?" Abby protested innocently.

"Like you're checking me out!"

Abby burst out laughing, "Don't be ridiculous!" she gasped, her laughter breaking through the tension between them.

James couldn't help himself and found himself cracking up too, not entirely sure why he was laughing but unable to stop himself from joining in with Abby's infectious giggling.

"You're one crazy lady!" James commented, rubbing his stubble with his fingertips.

"I know! I'm often told that!" Abby confessed as she descended into fits of laughter again.

"I've had 3 coffees in here now," Abby admitted, "I think I've gone a bit hyper!" she said, trying to regain some composure.

There was a loud bang from the doorway as Gino stumbled in through it and smashed into a wooden carving hanging on the wall opposite.

"Gino!" Paolo rushed over, cupping the young man's face in his hands before pulling him close for a big hug. Gino descended into tears almost immediately, speaking quickly in Spanish between huge, teary sobs.

Abby rushed over to help console the young man, not knowing what else to do and feeling extremely awkward sitting at the table watching the scene. Paolo explained that Gino had been questioned for hours and felt as if they had tried to coerce him into admitting his guilt at killing Mrs Cook. Abby gasped and looked over at James, who was now standing, but was hesitant to come over, given his role in this whole sorry saga.

"I thought you said Gino wasn't a suspect?" Abby accused, walking back over to James.

"I don't think I said any such thing." James explained lightly. "I said they would question him because it was he who was at the restaurant when Mrs Cook entered; I explained that to you Abby. If Gino is innocent then I can assure you he has nothing to worry about. We do have other people we are looking into."

"Like who?" Abby asked.

"You know I can't reveal details about an ongoing police investigation Abby."

"I know" Abby sighed, trying to make sense of her feelings. "I just feel bad, Gino was just putting his life back together. I just would hate to this be the catalyst for him throwing it all away again." Abby explained.

James smiled, never had he met anyone who put so much faith and energy into people they barely knew. "You know, if he's done as well as you say then he will get over this and he will get right back on track. It's unfortunate that when you've made your presence known to police then they have you in their sights. It's not a vindictive thing, it's just that they know you, they need to start somewhere, and they need to make sure offenders aren't reoffending, as harsh as that may be."

Abby glanced back at Gino, who was now sitting nursing a beer and being comforted by Paolo's wife. James was right, Abby acknowledged. There was nothing she could do, and while it was harsh that Gino felt so bad, she did see why the police had interrogated him. The way out of this for everyone would be to find out the real circumstances around Mrs Cook's death.

James touched Abby's arm gently and motioned to the door with his head. "Come on," he said "I think we should probably leave them to it."

While James left some money on the table for all the coffees Abby caught Paolo's eye and gave a little wave. They left the bar and Abby fell into step next to James, as they walked up towards the hotel. James walked Abby to her hotel room before glancing at his watch and making his excuses, almost running away.

MURDER IN MENORCA

CHAPTER SEVEN

The boys were inside when Abby walked into the apartment, getting their paddle boards ready for yet another adventure on the bright blue waters of the Mediterranean Sea. Abby told them about Gino and how upset he had been as she knew the boys had grown fond of him.

Luke wanted to go down to the restaurant straightaway and check on him, but Abby told him to wait for a while, until Gino wasn't so caught up in the emotion of it.

"You know, anyone could have done it." Will chimed in. "From what I've heard that old biddy wasn't exactly a barrel of fun."

"Well she was over 80 Will!" Abby defended poor Mrs Cook.

"Yes but she was mean. She was definitely mean to the staff anyway, from what the lads down at the beach say." Will defended his outburst.

"What do you mean?" asked Abby, wondering whether Will could be talking about some of those other suspects James had referred to.

"He's right Mum," chimed in Luke. "Franco, one of the waiters, said she was always moaning about staff and rubbing people up the wrong way. She was like the female version of that guy you like in that TV show, Victor Meldrew."

Abby laughed, she couldn't help herself. "Mrs Meldrew!?" she giggled, before slapping her hand over her mouth, "That's an awful thing to say," feeling quite guilty for speaking so meanly about someone so recently deceased.

"Imagine having her as a Mum!" Will said.

"She might have been a lovely Mum," Abby found herself defending Mrs Cook again, "Besides, who knows what her children turned out like. Maybe that's why she became so bitter and mean, maybe her children were a massive disappointment, or did something horrible." Abby looked pointedly at her boys, inferring in her look that if they even dared to do anything horrible....

"Honestly Mother!" Luke exhaled. "I think you got lucky with us, we're pretty cool, aren't we Will?"

"Absolutely!" Will agreed, smiling.

"Ha!" Abby exclaimed. "Yeah, you guys are pretty cool, but only cos I made you that way!"

"Whatever Mum!" the boys chimed up together.

Luke glanced at his phone, "Come on, we're gonna be late. We're meeting some of the lads down at the beach."

"What, you haven't got any other gossip you want to share with me?" asked Abby, keen to learn more about Mrs Cook and her behaviour to see whether she could get any hints about who the other suspects were.

"Nope," called out Will as he grabbed the boards and headed for the door.

"Unless you count the cleaner the old biddy got sacked the other day!?" added Luke, running down the steps and heading off for the beach road.

"The what!?" shouted Abby after them. But they had gone, off to play in the waves. She couldn't blame them really, they were on holiday after all, and what else do you do on holiday other than enjoy yourself. Which is what she should be doing, not trying to solve a crime she had no business in getting involved in.

However, if Mrs Cook had had a cleaner fired, then that meant one more person with a motive. And if there was one, there could be more. Which could be very good news for Gino, particularly if he wasn't the only one with the means to kill.

CAT PRESTON

CHAPTER EIGHT

The next morning, resolved to try and find out more about the sacked cleaner, Abby headed down to reception to have a word with Gina, the friendly receptionist, and see if she could shed some light on this new development. As she turned the corner of the building into the reception area however, she caught sight of James, standing casually against the reception desk, chatting animatedly with Gina.

An overwhelming feeling of jealousy swept over Abby as she stood back and pushed herself against the wall, making sure James didn't catch sight of her. Turning swiftly and seething inside, Abby stalked off in the direction of the beach, struggling to withhold her emotions. What was James doing here again? And why was he chatting so nicely to Gina? Was this part of his act? Abby wondered, suddenly feeling stupid for having feelings for such an obvious ladies man.

Lost in her own thoughts she didn't see Daniel, the travel rep, until she bumped into the board he was carrying.

"Miss Tennant" Daniel smiled warmly. "Is everything okay?"

"Just avoiding the police!" Abby admitted gruffly.

"You and me both," Daniel admitted. "They had me down the station for questioning yesterday as someone reported that Mrs Cook and I had had an altercation." Daniel ruffled his fingers through his hair distractedly, while hopping about from foot to foot. He looked like he was ready to take off at any moment.

"And did you do it?" Abby winked conspiratorially.

Abby got the response she wanted, as Daniel laughed at her cheeky comment. "They had to let me go eventually after realising that the likelihood of me committing murder because an elderly lady kept complaining about silly nonsense was extreme to say the least."

"I wouldn't worry; they seem to be questioning everyone!" Abby sighed.

"That's true." Daniel agreed. "I wouldn't mind so much, but I rather liked the old dear. I was here last year when she was here too; apparently she comes every year, though I've no idea why given the amount of complaining she does about the place."

"She complained last year but still came back to this specific hotel?" Abby asked incredulously. Why would you come back if you hadn't enjoyed yourself? Abby wondered.

"I think it was a hobby of hers. Mrs Meldrew I used to call her."

Abby laughed. "That's the exact same way my sons described her. She must have a bit of a reputation then hey!?"

"She was a cantankerous old biddy," Daniel admitted. "But she seemed much more on edge this year. I don't know, maybe she'd just got a year older and so was a year grumpier, but I don't remember her being as bad as she was this year."

"Don't you find that memories fade though and don't seem as bad when you look back?" Abby asked.

"I guess," Daniel agreed, "But still, I could have sworn something was eating away at her. Sometimes when you caught her she was all smiles and full of compliments, and then other times just the mere sound of your breathing would set her off on one of her rants. Completely unpredictable," Daniel looked off into space for a minute, as if remembering the last interaction she had with her, before adding "like a hurricane really."

"Wow! That bad!?" Abby asked.

"It wasn't her, it was something bothering her. I told the police I thought something was up but they didn't seem to take a blind bit of notice." Daniel looked past Abby then, "Talking of which," he said, "I'm going to make a move before the English one nabs me for more questioning. And with that Daniel grabbed his board and made his way to the events hall.

James approached just as Daniel scarpered with his board. "He was in a hurry," James commented.

"Running away from you I suspect," Abby stared at James, unsure how to broach this exchange. She'd decided to treat him like a teenage boy, what with his moods, up and down like a yo-yo. She could never tell how he was going to start out, and it put her on edge. If this was his idea of game playing he could play it by himself as she had no time for it, and would have no time for him if he kept it up.

"What were you two chatting about anyway?" James enquired.

"Why? You jealous?" Abby retorted, deciding on the cheeky approach.

James reddened before straightening himself up, puffing out his chest and flexing his muscles. Abby wondered if he knew what he was doing.

"Are you preening?" she asked cheekily.

"What!?" James coughed.

"You are aware that you're standing right in front of me puffing your chest out at me and flexing your muscles right?" she squinted through the sunlight before raising her hand to her forehead to block out the sun.

"Are you kidding me?" James said. "I come over here to say hi and you accuse me of behaving like some sort of peacock!?"

Abby burst out laughing. "A peacock?! Ha!"

Then she doubled over howling as James did a little peck dance especially for her. "Now this is peacock-y," he smiled, "No?"

Abby couldn't talk she was laughing so hard, and her infectious laugh caught James in its sights and grabbed hold of him, tickling him so hard he burst out laughing himself.

They were both so loud they started to attract the attention of people milling about, so Abby tried to reel herself in, but found it really difficult as each time she did James did a little peacock move, before breaking into laughter himself.

Finally catching her breath, Abby said "Will you shush, you're causing a scene!"

James looked around aghast, "You don't think anyone seen my peacock moves do you?" causing Abby to crease up in hysterics again.

James grabbed Abby's arm and they both moved off toward the beach road.

"I don't even know why I'm laughing," James admitted. "This all started with you making fun of me!"

Abby snorted, "You did look ridiculous!" she laughed.

"You know, I was not flexing my pecks or whatever it was you think I was doing," James moaned.

Abby rolled her eyes animatedly. "Whatever, Mr Oh-so-smooth!"

"Nothing wrong with being smooth" grinned James.

"You know this isn't the way I envisaged dedicated police officers acting?" Abby teased.

"Who said I was dedicated?" James winked. "And besides, we're only human, we're allowed a bit of a laugh occasionally. I just thought you looked like you could do with cheering up."

"Really?" Abby looked at him intensely. "I think it was the other way round. I think you needed a laugh and you knew I'd accommodate."

"Maybe. You're easy to talk to. Sometimes you just want to chat rather than putting on the whole police persona." James admitted.

Abby looked up then, only just taking note of where they were, "Oh!" she exclaimed. "How the heck did we get here!?" She hadn't realised all the while she'd been mocking James, so caught up in enjoying their easy conversation, they'd been walking while talking and suddenly found themselves on the beach.

"Well fancy that!" said James, "We might as well get some lunch while we're down here hey?" he suggested as he directed Abby towards a little seafood restaurant on the beachfront.

"I don't remember saying 'Yes'!" Abby warned.

"Come on, you owe me. For all the teasing. You've made me all self-conscious now. Plus are you really going to let a lonely old policeman eat by himself?" James pleaded, smiling all the while.

"Ha! As if!" Abby looked at the restaurant, one she hadn't been in yet. "You know, okay, but only because I haven't tried this one yet." She smiled.

"Oh, charmed I'm sure. Nothing to do with my company then?" James teased.

"You'll do as much as the next," Abby shot right back.

James held the door open for Abby as they walked through the restaurant, and asked the waiter if they could have a table outside. Abby followed the waiter through the cosy restaurant and out to the balcony area, where little tables were perfectly set up to take advantage of the stunning sea views. Sparkling white linen tablecloths adorned the tables, with little crystal vases with a single yellow flower sitting on top. James asked if Abby fancied a drink and she went for a cool, crisp glass of chardonnay, while James chose a lime and soda.

"You do surprise me!" Abby commented on James's drink choice.

"Well, technically I'm on duty. But there's nothing in the rule book that says I can't take time out for lunch. I just can't drink," James explained.

"We better make this a quick lunch then hey?" Abby teased.

Abby went with the house special of freshly caught filleted fish, smothered in a delicious buttery garlic and lemon sauce with a side of crisp salad and a decent helping of extremely tasty chips. James went for the other house special...steak.

"How can you have steak when we're at a seafood restaurant?" Abby cried incredulously. "You've gotta think their fish dishes are going to be 100 times better than anything else given that's their specialty?"

James just laughed, "Sorry, but I'm really craving red meat for some reason. It just sounded too good to turn down."

Abby laughed, "Flintstone!"

"Flintstone?" James raised an eyebrow.

"Yep. Flintstone. As in Fred. Or in laymen's terms, how about caveman?" Abby teased. She was getting good at this flirty teasing thing, she thought.

"You know it's not really considered very good manners to tease someone about their choice of meal. How would you like it if I teased you about yours?" James grinned.

"I'm really just wishing you'd ordered a beer now as well, so I could firmly stick you in the English stereotypical man column." Abby hadn't had so much fun in ages. The stress of her marriage breaking down and then struggling to raise her two boys by herself had left her with little time to enjoy the simple things in life others enjoyed, like dating. Dating? Abby thought, shoot, is this a date?

"Why've you suddenly gone quiet?" James asked, "What have you just thought?"

Abby shifted uncomfortably in her chair. Did she ask whether this was a date? If it was, would she need to ask? Of course it wasn't a date, she told herself, it's just two people having lunch together at lunchtime, nothing more. With flirting. Definitely with flirting, but did the flirting make it a date? She hadn't dated since, well, since she'd dated her husband.

James touched Abby's hand gently, and somehow caught her eye, dragging it up to meet his by some strange mystical power she just had to learn. "Hey," he smiled as he rubbed his thumb gently against the back of her hand, "what's going on in there?"

He's got such kind eyes, Abby thought, feeling almost spellbound by them. She blinked, breaking the spell, and moved her hand back, placing it on her lap. James sat back in his chair, waiting for her to explain her sudden change.

"Sorry," Abby shared, "I just suddenly thought, this is the first time I've had a nice meal with a man in I don't even know how long. It just kinda threw me."

"Really?" James asked. "How long ago did your marriage break up then?"

"Years ago." Abby laughed nervously. "I kinda got into a routine of just concentrating on the boys and my job and was happy just going out with friends. I didn't really look for anything else." Why on earth did she feel the need to tell this man all her most embarrassing secrets. Of course from that he could absolutely guess how long it had been since she'd slept with anyone, god how embarrassing. Abby shrunk down in her seat, feeling as if her cheeks were going to explode with the heat radiating through them.

"So you've not dated since the break-up of your marriage then?" James asked, fighting the urge to lean over the table and kiss her, seeing how fidgety and embarrassed she was discussing her love life, or lack thereof.

"Nope!" Abby managed.

"Me neither really." James confessed.

"Really?" Abby asked, intrigued, and feeling a little better about her own situation.

"Really. We broke up when my daughter, Jen, was 10 and she took it pretty hard. I decided to forgo the whole dating scene for a bit as I saw how upset it made her. Then when she was

MURDER IN MENORCA

16 she started asking me why I'd never dated anyone else. Her mum was already re-married by this point so I really didn't have any excuse. Then she started trying to set me up on dates!"

"No!" Abby leaned in closer, intrigued. "And, how did that go?"

"Awful!" James confessed, a look of pain on his face as he recalled the couple of dates he'd let himself be talked into.

James noticed Abby had come right back out of her shell again, and realised, not for the first time, that he really enjoyed spending time with her, even if that meant he had to share all his embarrassing secrets as well.

"You really want to know about my dating life?" James warned.

"Are you kidding me?" Abby asked, "I'm riveted! I already know this is gonna be good from the look on your face."

"Cheers!" James grimaced. "Okay, so first she decided that her best friend's mum, who'd just broken up with a long-term boyfriend, would be absolutely perfect for me. Girls can be very sly you know."

"Ha! What did she do?"

"She told me she'd love it if we could go for a picnic together. She wanted to talk about what she was going to do after school. I thought it sounded like a lovely idea and was really excited about the whole thing. I bought everything from the M&S Food Hall in town, all their little delicious but tiny picnic

51

treats, and walked down to the local park to meet her, only she wasn't alone. Her friend had done the exact same thing. So there we were, four of us tucking into this picnic, which would have been perfect for two, but was pathetic for four, so right off I felt like a right idiot. Then the 2 of them scarpered, apparently they wanted to go and play on the swings. They were 16. What a load of rubbish."

"Clever girl," Abby commented, leaning closer in. "So..."

"So I ask one question: "What do you do for a living?" thinking it would be the safest one to ask, and she turns on the waterworks straightaway. I mean it was instantaneous. And it wasn't pretty. I sat there for over 40 minutes trying to console her while she sobbed and blew her nose and wailed. It was excruciating. The worst thing was there seemed to be a constant stream of people walking by and they all kept giving me really evil looks, of course she was oblivious to everything but her own misery. It was one of the most cringeworthy moments of my life."

Abby sat in her seat, almost doubled over from laughing.. "I can just picture your face!" she snorted.

"I was not impressed. The girls materialised after about 40 minutes, Jenny's friend running to her mum's aid and giving me a look that could kill vampires. Even Jenny was looking at me like I was a madman."

"Oh my god, stop!" Abby pleaded, her stomach aching from laughing so much.

"Well, I'm glad you find it funny!" James playfully kicked Abby's foot under the table.

"So, was that the worst one?" Abby asked after getting her breath back.

"Nope!" James stated bluntly.

"You're kidding?"

"I wish I was. She put me on a dating site, and got me a date with "a looker" – her words not mine. Turned out the looker was a guy who liked dressing as a woman." James confessed.

"A cross-dresser? You? And a cross-dresser?" Abby couldn't take much more, she laughed so hard she was now coughing but she motioned with her hand for James to continue.

"Yeah it didn't get far. He made me for a copper almost straightaway. But we had a couple of beers and joked about it. He was actually a pretty decent guy."

"Just not your type, no?" Abby chuckled.

The waiter came over with their food, looking curiously at Abby, as she struggled to control her laughing fit. He nervously placed the meals down and then made a hasty retreat.

"We must look crazy," Abby commented, cocking her head in the direction of the retreating waiter, who was making his way to 3 other restaurant workers, all looking over in the direction of their table and whispering. "You're sitting there all straight-faced and I can barely talk for laughing. I wonder what they must be saying about us."

"They probably think you're being ludicrously mean to me or something," James stated matter-of-factly.

"Ha!" Abby scoffed before taking a bite of her fish. "Oh my god, this is delicious!" She put a bit of the fish onto her fork and then shoved it in James direction, "You've got to try this," she said.

The mmmmm sound that came from his throat made her toes curl and her stomach fill with bubbles, all popping simultaneously and making her heart flutter dangerously fast. She had never been so turned on by a murmur before.

James hadn't seemed to notice her reaction to him though, savouring the fish before tucking into his steak.

"As good?" Abby asked.

"It's good, but I wish I'd gone with yours. That's amazing!" James admitted.

"Told you," Abby grinned, feeling wonderfully cocky.

Over coffee, the talk turned to the case and Abby asked James about the cleaner and whether they'd interviewed her. She came up with some pretty good scenarios about how a cleaner could get revenge for getting fired, completely ignoring James's eye rolling as each scenario got worse than the next. Then Abby asked why Daniel had been interviewed.

James found himself getting annoyed at himself as feelings of jealousy bubbled up inside him after the mere mention of the holiday rep, Daniel; a man who kept himself in much better shape than James did, and seemed to have a near constant circle of women and girls surrounding him as he flaunted his half naked body around the resort.

"You know I can't divulge any information about the case," he warned Abby. "But we have to rule out anyone and everyone who is brought to our attention, and if a disagreement is reported we would be remiss to investigate."

"So who else have you interviewed?" Abby tried.

James rolled his eyes dramatically. "Am I going to get bored of repeating the same phrase?"

Abby echoed his favourite saying: "I can't talk about the case" in as low a voice as she could, trying to mimic his gestures but probably looking like a right numpty instead.

"Not sure about the impression, but you get the message. And stop involving yourself in the case would you!? You're either going to end up getting me or you in trouble. We don't know what we're dealing with here, and I don't want you getting caught in something that could be dangerous, okay?"

"Okay," Abby agreed, feeling like a naughty schoolgirl being scolded.

Not wanting to give up looking into the case Abby could understand how James felt, particularly if anything she did could interfere with his job, and potentially get him into trouble with his bosses.

James paid the bill and thanked Abby for lunch.

"I should be the one thanking you." Abby countered. "Thank you. It was delicious. And fun. Definitely one of the best lunches I've had in a long, long time" she smiled, genuinely meaning every word.

"I'm glad my embarrassing stories entertained you so much," James said. "So what are your plans for the rest of the day then?"

"I don't know. I was going to go and find one of these undiscovered hidden beach gems I've been hearing so much about."

"Sounds lovely. I found a gorgeous little cove the other week. It's a really beautiful island." James said. He looked at his watch and looked up in amazement "You know, our lunch lasted almost 3 hrs!?" he asked.

"Really?" Abby grinned, "Time must have flown cos I'm such good company."

"Hmmmm," James drummed his finger against his chin.

"Oi!" Abby grumbled.

"So is it just eating you're good company for or is it other things too?" James teased.

"Obviously I'm just great company all round," Abby beamed sarcastically.

"So if I asked if I could join your beach hunt?" James suggested with a note of hesitancy, unsure whether Abby would accept his invitation or not.

"Don't you have to get back to work?" Abby asked, thinking how lovely it would be to have someone accompany her. "Of course, if you don't then I'd love some company. It kinda gets lonely exploring by yourself and having no-one to share it with," she confessed.

James's smile said it all. "Nah! I'll call into the office and take a half day. I can't waste an opportunity like this now, can I?"

CAT PRESTON

CHAPTER NINE

James offered to drive so they strolled back to the hotel where his car was parked. Abby ran into her apartment to grab a couple of towels and slip her swimming costume on under a summer dress and they were off. James drove to his recently discovered cove, excited to show Abby his find. Ten minutes later and James was parking up at the side of the road.

"That was quick," Abby commented.

"It's a pretty small island. And there are loads of these little coves hidden all around it. This is the one I was telling you about the other day."

James jumped out and made his way around the car, opening the passenger side door before Abby had even gathered her bag and bits together.

"Why, thank you!" exclaimed Abby dramatically.

"Nothing wrong with a bit of door opening," James smiled.

"I couldn't agree more." They grabbed their bits from the car and headed down a little path.

"They've got some really rickety, old steps to get you down to the cove but they seemed pretty safe last time." James warned.

James took Abby's beach bag and they wandered down the steps slowly, finally making it to the beach, where Abby kicked off her flip flops and sunk her feet into the soft, golden sand.

"Wow!" she exclaimed, looking around. The cove was set between two hulking great rocks with smaller rocks edging into the sea. The beach looked barely touched, and Abby made her way straight down to the water, which lapped gently against the rocks. The blue of the sea was beguiling and she couldn't help but walk out into it a little way, until the water lapped against her ankles, the warmth of it surprising her.

"Like it?" James asked from behind her, his voice husky with feeling.

"It's amazing," Abby breathed sultrily. James inclined his head towards the sea and asked "Fancy a dip?" holding out a pair of swimming shorts he'd fished out from the boot of his car.

"I'd love to!" Abby agreed, before hesitantly looking around for somewhere a tiny bit more private to take off her dress and adjust her costume.

Abby looked over at James self-consciously, not really wanting to peel off her clothes in front of him.

Noticing her discomfort James pointed to his shorts, "I have no way of getting these on without stripping down to nothing, so unless you want to see my milky white bum how about we both turn around until the other says 'Ready'?" James suggested.

Abby smiled appreciatively and turned, laying the two towels down on the sand and peeling her dress off and throwing it on top of them. She adjusted her costume to make sure nothing inappropriate had escaped and then shouted "Ready!"

"Hold on a minute!" James protested. "I'm naked as the day I was born here!"

"Really?" asked Abby suggestively, desperate to turn around and have a peek.

"Peek if you want, but you'll only see my hairy butt crack," James warned cheekily.

"Hmmm, maybe I'll just wait until you're ready," Abby said. James loved that he could hear the smile in her voice without even needing to see it.

"Ok," he touched her arm gently and she spun around and pulled an exaggeratedly disappointed face, "Oooh," she moaned, "I was hoping you'd be wearing some tighty-whitey speedos or something," she joked.

"I left them ones in the car," James fired back. "I could always go and get them?"

"Nah! You look fine as you are," she commented. And he did. James was wearing black shorts that finished a couple of inches above the knee, just managing to show off his tight upper leg muscles. His legs were hairy and toned, and his upper body revealed a deliciously hairy chest that Abby had to fight a reaction to curl her fingers into. His stomach was a little tubby but he looked extremely sexy standing there, looking ready to pounce.

"When you're quite finished?" he teased.

"What?" Abby played the innocence card.

"You were blatantly checking me out!" James said. "I felt like a piece of meat!"

"I was not!" Abby argued, although she already knew her damn cheeks were giving her away.

Abby was wearing a cobalt blue swimming costume that made her pale skin shimmer in the sun. James stirred deep inside, unable to control his body's reaction to her, and decided the best course of action would be to make a beeline to the sea and hide his attraction to her.

"Race you!" he called out as he ran towards the gentle waves.

Abby wrapped her arms self-consciously across her body, subconsciously trying to hide her body from James's view, as she made her way down to the sea. James dived into the frothy whiteness of the cascading waves before turning to see Abby still making her way down the beach. He noticed her body language, wondering why she felt the need to hide her amazingly attractive body behind her arms. Surely most women would give their right arm to look like Abby did at her age? he thought.

As she joined him in the sea he couldn't help but say, "You look amazing!" to which Abby looked more than a little embarrassed and flicked off his compliment with a wave.

James looked at her, studying her face, trying to work her out, she seemed so confident in herself but didn't seem to know how to handle compliments. He wondered what kind of an idiot her ex-husband must have been to let someone like Abby go.

"The water is almost as warm as a heated pool," Abby said, tilting her head back into the sea.

"Do you want to swim out a bit?" James asked.

Abby looked at him guiltily, "I have a confession," she started, "I might not be the best person to be here with for this."

"Why?" James asked, thinking he wouldn't want to be here with anyone else.

"I kind of can't swim," she said quietly.

James laughed softly.

"It's not funny," Abby said, smiling despite herself. She loved how no matter what he said James didn't make her feel stupid, or concerned about admitting things about herself that she hated admitting to others.

"Do you want me to teach you?" he asked with a big grin.

"Well, I kind of can, and I kind of can't," Abby explained. "I can swim if I can reach the bottom with my feet. As soon as I can't I panic. And then turn into a whimpering, spluttering mess. It's not pretty."

"So is it the not reaching the bottom or the going under bit that you don't like?" James asked kindly.

"Both really. I hate it when my face goes under because I think I try to breathe, and then I just ended up coughing up water. And I just don't like the feeling of not being able to reach the bottom. And then there's the whole Jaws thing," Abby continued.

James laughed, "The Jaws thing?"

"Yup. It's an unexplained phenomena." Abby shrugged her shoulders, "I can be absolutely fine, and then suddenly I think about sharks or jellyfish and just freak out."

"How on earth did you raise those two water-loving boys?" James asked, incredulously.

"Well, I'm not putting my stupid fears onto them now am I?!" Abby explained. "I took them to swimming lessons, made sure they were absolutely able to hold their own in the water before I'd let them go further than me, and I panicked like mad obviously."

"So I've found your Achilles heel then?" he asked.

"My what?"

"The thing you're most scared of." James explained.

"One of them maybe," Abby countered.

"Really?" James said, surprise evident in his voice, "And are you going to share the others?"

"All in good time," Abby smiled, thinking of every parent's one overriding fear, the fear of anything happening to their child.

James cocked his head at the intensity of her gaze. "You amaze me," he admitted. "You're like every single emotion all tied up in one big bow. And that's the best way I can describe it."

Now it was Abby's turn to laugh. "Aren't we all?" she questioned.

"Not as evidently all out in the open as you," James explained.

"Oh." Abby didn't quite know how to take that one. Was it meant to be a compliment or not? Personally, she liked that she expressed her emotions when she felt them, what would be the point in bottling them up all the time? James noticed the skin between her eyebrows crinkle up as she considered his answer.

"I love that about you," he blurted out, before trying to back pedal. God, what was he saying? Who used the word 'love' on a kinda first date, jeez, he was definitely losing his touch as he got older. But then, the hell with it, he thought. "Yep, I do love that about you," he repeated. "It's so nice to actually know what someone is feeling without having to guess. People know where they are with you Abby, not everyone can do that. I think it's one of the nicest things about you." Okay, he thought, now enough sloppy stuff. He suddenly felt like he was in an episode of Dawson's Creek.

"Oh my god," Abby teased, "You're blushing. I've just seen you blush!" Abby smiled happily, achievement all over her face. "Was it showering me with compliments that made you blush so?" Abby grinned widely before kicking her feet in the air and floating on her back. "Don't let me drift out, will you?" she called out.

"Never." James said, emotion tugging on his voice.

He flipped himself onto his back and moved closer to Abby, them both floating side by side, only their hands gently moving with the waves to keep them afloat.

"I can't remember the last time I felt so relaxed," James said softly.

Abby turned her head slowly to the side to try and catch a glance of James's face, before touching his hand ever so lightly and saying, "Me neither. It feels wonderful."

The floating part lasted the whole of two minutes before Abby noticed a big wave crashing towards them. "Watch out!" she shouted as she got herself vertical and made a jump for the top of the wave.

James was too slow and the wave crashed over him, sending him crashing towards the beach. He finally jumped up, shaking the water off him like some sort of aquatic sea god, or at least that's what Abby imagined sea gods would look like as they rose from the waves.

Abby reached him at the same time as a second wave came crashing over them, this time taking them both further towards the beach. They ended up splashing down into the shallows of the water, with Abby wiping the water out of her eyes and spluttering as James came face to face with a jellyfish. Shooting backwards he pointed the jellyfish out to Abby, who squirmed and retreated to the safety of the beach, collapsing into the sand with a dramatic plop. James followed suit, and they sat down with a dramatic plop, laughing. They stayed there for a while, letting the waves lap against their feet and chatting animatedly about the island.

"I can't believe you almost got stung by a jellyfish," Abby commented, casually stroking her fingers down James's upper arm, where the jellyfish almost collided with James.

James laughed. "You reacted much better than I was expecting."

"Well that was because it was going for you and not me!" Abby grinned.

"Do you want to go again?" James asked, nodding his head toward the sea.

"Come on then," Abby agreed, jumping up and heading back towards the waves.

As they stood in the water, playing amongst the white frothy waves like kids, Abby felt about a decade younger than she was. She edged out further into the sea, letting the now gentle waves wash over her, almost feeling like they were cleansing her. James moved closer to her, wanting to close the gap between them, getting close enough to reach out and touch her just as another wave threatened to envelope them.

"Careful!" he pointed towards the impending wave and they jumped at the same time, the wave missing them this time and Abby whooped in triumph. James laughed and found himself pulling her towards him. Abby didn't stop him, and with her body pressed up against his, he bent down and kissed her. What had meant to be a simple kiss created a spark so strong they both came up gasping for air.

James looked down into Abby's eyes, desperate to kiss her again, his hands wrapping themselves protectively around her waist. Abby bridged the tiny gap between them, her hand curling around James's neck and pulling his head down towards hers, their lips meeting again in a tantalisingly delicious kiss. She parted her lips, allowing his tongue to enter her mouth, a murmur escaping from her throat as their legs became entwined.

They didn't notice the wave until it was upon them, sending them crashing towards the beach for a second time that day. Their legs were pulled from under them, and Abby felt James's arms tighten around her, pushing her up to the surface as he went under. They landed sprawled together on the sand, the waves swaying against their bodies, James on the floor and Abby hovering over him.

Abby had no words. This might have been the most romantic moment of her life if at that precise moment her leg hadn't seized up in a muscle spasm and she didn't have water plastering her hair over her eyes.

She rolled to the side, sitting up and stretching out her leg whilst simultaneously wiping her hair away from her face and coughing out the half litre of seawater that had made its way into her lungs.

"Are you okay?" James asked, sitting up.

"Yes, I've just got cramp." Abby grimaced.

James moved himself around so he was sitting facing Abby, her legs sprawled out between them.

"Where?" James asked, motioning toward her leg.

Abby pointed to the pinched spot and he gently massaged her leg, his warm hands splayed against her lower leg, sending little shockwaves coursing up her body as they moved over her skin.

Abby let her head tilt back, her eyes closing as she let herself be swept up in the moment. Wow, did he give a good massage, she thought before her thoughts headed south and she had to stop herself from thinking anymore.

"That was amazing!" Abby said breathlessly, her eyes opening up and then straining against the sun.

James leaned back, pretending to assess her leg but really just taking the opportunity to admire the view. "Feeling better?" he asked, his hand still laying on Abby's leg. She twitched as he ran his fingers up to her knee, cupping it in his hand before slowly tickling behind her knee and tracing his fingers back down to her ankle bone.

"You are something else!" James said, struggling to maintain his composure. He moved his body to sit next to Abby's then, their hands touching as they steadied themselves in the sand. Abby looked over, watching James's chest move up and down with his breath, imagining what it would feel like to lay her head there, listening to his heartbeat.

As she pulled her eyes up and away from noticing how his chest hairs curled up to meet his throat, she found herself looking into his eyes. James leant over, closing the gap between them. His hand reached out, cupping her face, his fingers delicately stroking her chin as his lips were drawn to hers, tasting the salt of the water on them.

His hand dropped to her upper arm, tracing patterns in her skin with his fingertips as his body edged ever closer, until there was no gap between them at all. Abby moved then, wanting to be even closer, and hooking a leg over him she lifted herself up, sitting astride him and gazing down into his gruffly handsome face

"Abigail," James moaned, sending tingles of pleasure throughout Abby's body. The way his voice flicked over the sounds in her name made her heart skip a beat.

She lay both hands on either side of his face as their kiss became deeper, both losing themselves in each other. James's hands lay on Abby's lower back, encouraging her towards him, wanting to feel her body glued against his. Abby felt his hard body moving intimately against hers and knew, if she didn't stop now she wouldn't be able to later. With one last final, urgent kiss she pulled herself away and collapsed next to his heaving body, spent.

James turned to look at her, breathless with passion, his chest heaving as he tried to slow his breathing. She could feel his eyes moving across her body, could feel the heat as they moved up towards her face, and when they did she met them with her own intense gaze, her cheeks flush with desire.

James didn't know what to say, he was lost for words, which was a new sensation for him. He'd never experienced a kiss like it before, unsure where all the emotion and heat and intensity of it came from. At last he simply said, "Was that just me or was that....?"

"Amazing?" Abby finished for him, a slow, sexy smile spreading across her face.

"Yes," he said, his hand finding hers, their fingers interlocking. "I...just...Wow!" he finished, still trying to control the urges that swept over him. Abby leaned her head against his arm, still breathing heavily, and finally allowed herself to reach up and tangle her fingers into his chest hair.

"I've been wanting to do that all day," she confessed.

"Which bit?" asked James, wrapping an arm around Abby's shoulders, his hand falling against her lower back, and pulling her against him, wanting to keep her forever close.

Abby looked up at him, "This bit," she said, motioning towards her fingers, which were now splayed against his chest, somewhat hidden inside the mass of curls. "But I am absolutely not complaining about all the other bits," she smiled mischievously.

"You don't think I should wax it all off then?" James dipped his head towards his chest.

"Hell no!" exclaimed Abby, reaching over with her free hand and swiping James's other hand, sending them both smacking into the sand.

"Ow!" James moaned. Abby nestled her head into the space between his shoulder and his chest, and sighed pleasurably, cocking a leg over and letting it come to rest in between his. "Oh, now that's better," James admitted, thoroughly enjoying being snuggled into. His hand came to rest against Abby's belly, as if it had always belonged there.

They lay there for a while, enjoying the sound of the waves lapping against the sand and the stillness of the air until Abby got thirsty and made a move towards her bag. It was the cue to head back to reality and as they packed up and got ready to leave the beach James touched Abby lightly on the shoulder. "I've had a fantastic day," he said, as she turned to face him.

"Me too," Abby smiled up at him, before folding her arms around him and inhaling the smell of him deep inside her, trying to intoxicate herself with it so she would never forget it. She knew this moment wouldn't last forever, but as long as it did last she was going to absorb every precious ounce of pleasure from it.

James stroked her hair, breathing in Abby's scent and wondering whether he could prolong the day any further.

"Drink?" he asked gingerly.

"Sure." Abby nodded enthusiastically, not wanting to part company either.

"Come on then," he said, grabbing her hand and making his way to the car, trying to mask the emotion he felt. As they reached the car they both looked back at the beach, Abby noticing a bottle of sun tan lotion they had left behind. She nudged him and pointed, making to move toward the beach again, but James held out a hand, stopping her in her tracks, "Let me," he said. "I'll be 2 minutes," he called out as he started running down the slope they'd walked up, ignoring the rickety steps they'd used earlier.

Abby leaned against the car, watching him, marvelling at how much she liked him already, how it had taken this long for her to have such strong feelings about another man. James seemed to be the polar opposite of her ex. Yes, they both had strong, sturdy frames, but James used his completely differently. There was nothing threatening about James's demeanour, not that she had witnessed anyway. No underlying anger, or bitterness, nothing in fact that reminded her of her ex-husband. Thank god, Abby thought watching James as he reached the bottom of the slope and swept up the bottle in one hand before looking up and waving with the other. Even his little wave made Abby's heart skip a beat.

When James reached the top Abby already had her dress on, and was holding out a t-shirt she had found on the back seat of the car. James pulled on the t-shirt before opening the door for Abby. She stood on her tiptoes, and brushed his cheek with her lips before climbing in.

"Would you prefer to change before we go for a drink?" James asked, realising they were still in their swimwear.

"Absolutely!" Abby said, "I'm still technically in my swimsuit!"

MURDER IN MENORCA

CHAPTER TEN

James picked Abby up at her apartment at 8pm on the dot, dressed far more suitably in a pair of jeans and a short-sleeved checked shirt. Abby wore a simple yellow dress which perfectly complimented her sun-kissed skin and tousled brown curls. She wore simple slip-on sandals and carried her evening bag on her shoulder, her gold necklace catching the lights as they walked down towards the seafront.

"This might be a record for me," he admitted.

"What's that?" Abby asked.

"Two dates in one day! Especially as it's with the same woman!" he winked.

"Well play your cards right and you might even get a quick peck on the cheek at the end of it," Abby joked, linking her arm through James's.

They ended up walking up the hill and settled in a restaurant overlooking the bay, sipping raspberry mojitos and enjoying some Spanish tapas. Abby talked animatedly about her boys and James opened up about his daughter, Jenny, both longing to share their history with each other, and their most important history being their children.

James sat spellbound, listening to Abby regale him with stories of life with teenage boys, sharing similar stories with her of his own childhood, and remembering his own Mum and how she fretted about him as much as Abby did about her two. He realised he missed being part of a family, having people worry about you and want to look after you.

Walking back up the hill after far too much food and maybe too many cocktails, Abby leaned her head against James's shoulder, hugging his arm tight to her. Not for the first time today did she feel like a silly schoolgirl again, caught up in the romance of a perfect day and not wanting to let it go.

"I've had a lovely day," she told James as they approached the hotel, "Thank you."

James stopped and gently pulled Abby round so she was facing him, cupping her face in his hands and gazing far into those beautiful brown eyes. "You make me feel young again," he confessed, laughing.

"I should do," Abby countered, "I'm at least 3 years younger than you, surely!?" her eyes glinting mischievously. James brushed his thumb against Abby's bottom lip before following it up with his mouth, their tongues uniting as if they'd been away from each other for far too long. Abby wrapped her arms around James's body, her hands resting on his upper back, feeling the strength beneath them.

"I can't come in," James said, his hand moving to the small of her back, his fingers doing a little dance there, making her spine tingle.

"I know," Abby groaned, knowing full well that if he did they would end up in her bed, and heaven only knew how she'd explain that one away in the morning to two nosey teenagers.

James walked Abby to her door, where they kissed again, neither one of them wanting the night to end.

"I'll see you tomorrow?" James asked.

"Well I won't be hard to find," Abby said, "I'll be nursing a hangover in the corner somewhere," she smiled, her hand touching his cheek and brushing against his stubble. She reached up for one last kiss, savouring the taste of him and the softness of his lips, drinking in the smell of him before she turned and opened the door to her apartment, blowing a kiss as she shut it.

James stood there for a moment, wondering how on earth he'd got to this point from where he'd been this morning. What a day, he thought as he headed back toward town and his apartment.

CAT PRESTON

CHAPTER ELEVEN

Abby woke the next morning with a huge smile on her face and buzzed around the apartment getting ready for the day. Luke was lying hungover on the couch, not quite able to move, which Abby would normally have moaned at him about but she was feeling so good she simply grabbed a blanket to drape over him and put some ibuprofen and a glass of water on the coffee table, within easy reach.

"Thanks Mum," Luke croaked. "You look happy," he managed a half smile before turning over and burrowing his head under the blanket. Will wasn't much better, although his behaviour was down to pure stroppy teenage boy syndrome. Abby opened the door to the second bedroom which the boys were sharing, and popped her head in whispering to Will, "Are you okay? Do you want to come down to breakfast?"

"What time is it?" groaned a voice from beneath the covers.

"It's 9am," Abby responded.

"Oh Mum!!! It's way too early! Wake me up at 11 would you, I have a date."

Abby walked into the room at that news and perched on the edge of the bed. "A date?" she asked inquisitively. She pulled the covers down just enough so she could see Will's face and slowly tickled his cheek until he opened one eye and batted her hand away. "Who's the date with?" she persisted.

"Oh Mum!! I didn't mean a date I meant I'm just meeting someone," Will tried to get out of revealing his personal life to his Mum, but he was too late and he knew it. He'd revealed a snippet and now he knew she wouldn't rest until she knew it all.

"Fine!" he said, lifting his head off the pillow. "I'm meeting a girl I got chatting to last night. She's from Manchester. She's the same age as me and she's cool, so don't go making a show of me will you!?"

Abby grinned, 'Kids!' she thought. "Now why would I make a show of you?" she challenged with just a hint of mischief in her voice. "What time are you meeting her?"

"At one," Will said, flopping his head back onto the pillow and closing his eyes.

Abby took that as the cue that this little conversation was over. She leaned over and planted a kiss on Wills cheek, which he promptly wiped off with the back of his hand.

"Love you!" she called out as she left the room.

"Love you too," she heard Will mumble before, "Oh Mum," he called out.

"Yes," Abby answered, popping her head back round the door.

"Could you bring me back a chocolate croissant and an orange? Please?" Will asked with a desperate lilt to his voice.

"I'll see." Abby called, knowing full well that the first thing she'd be grabbing when she hit the breakfast buffet was the croissant and orange.

Abby grabbed her bag and turned to leave when her eldest summoned her over with a croak. "Mum!" Luke barely managed.

Abby went over and ruffled his hair. He might be a legitimately grown adult now but he was still her baby, and she could still ruffle his hair if she wanted, no matter how much he protested.

"Can I get the same as Will? But can I have 2 oranges? And an orange ice lolly, you know how they cure hangovers."

"I'll see what I can do," Abby promised before finally escaping the room.

"Mum! I want an ice lolly too!" Will called out as Abby shut the door.

"Okay," she called back before almost running away before she got any more requests.

On her way to breakfast Abby stopped by the reception, wanting to ask about how the cleaner Mrs Cook got fired. However, when she asked about it the receptionist simply smiled and pointed to a woman walking past with a bucket in her hand, "You mean Margot?"

"I thought Mrs Cook had her fired?" Abby asked, confused.

"Well, she said she wanted her fired, but the manager wasn't going to fire our best cleaner just because Mrs Cook, god rest

MURDER IN MENORCA

her soul of course, had one of tizzy fits. No, he sent her to work on the other side of the hotel so Mrs Cook would be none the wiser," the receptionist winked conspiratorially.

"Do the police know that?" Abby asked.

"Oh yes," the receptionist confirmed. "That nice English one asked about it, he thought it was a great idea!" she smiled smugly.

"Oh, okay, well thank you," Abby muttered as she backed away from the reception.

James had known all along, and had let her tell the story about the fired cleaner, and let her go through all the scenarios she had offered up about how the cleaner might have been so annoyed she'd spiked Mrs Cook's drink. God, she felt foolish now. He must have been sitting there, trying not to laugh.

As Abby mulled over this latest development whilst eating her breakfast she started getting irritated, torn between rationalising why James wouldn't have told her about the cleaner, and livid that he'd let her warble on about it and hadn't bothered to tell her. She knew he couldn't discuss an ongoing case, but couldn't he have just told her that the cleaner had simply been moved? Abby couldn't explain why something so trivial would bother her so much, and yet it did. Was it because James had lied to her, but then he hadn't had he she thought, he'd just not said anything. And what was it to do with her anyway? her sensible side argued. But her feisty side was having none of it, she had been enjoying trying to figure out the mystery, thought she'd been doing quite

79

well in fact, but really she was just a novice, playing in the big boys field.

After going back to the room to check on the boys and deliver their breakfast and lollies Abby went for a swim to shake herself out of her ridiculous mood and then caught some rays on one of the sunbeds dotted around the pool. She chatted to some of the other guests and, after bumping into Eveline and Jane and catching them up on the sad news, agreed to meet them at Paolo's restaurant for a gossip and lunch.

She headed back to the room to find Luke had given up on the couch and had moved over to his bed, still feeling sorry for himself.

"Why don't you go and have a swim," Abby suggested, "It may liven you up a bit. At this rate it'll be getting dark again before you've even showered."

"That's alright," Luke said, "I'm not meeting the lads until teatime; I've got loads of time," pulling the covers up over his head to block out the sunlight.

"But you're missing all the sun!" Abby said, "You'll go home as pasty white as when you came."

"This is the first day I've been in bed this late Mum" Luke moaned.

"Right," Abby threatened, "If you don't get up and out within the next 30 minutes I'm going to drag you to lunch with me. I'm meeting Eveline and Jane."

"What? The old biddies? You need to find yourself some friends more your own age Mum!" Luke complained.

MURDER IN MENORCA

"I'll have you know they are very cool old biddies, thank you very much!" said Abby, feeling as if she'd had this conversation before. "Come on, I'm going to get changed, I want you up by the time I come back in."

Abby left the room to teenage grunts and groans, smiling as she went. He'd thank her later she knew, especially if he got a little bit of colour on those milky white legs.

CAT PRESTON

CHAPTER TWELVE

Having kicked Luke out into the sunshine and sent Will off on his date Abby wandered over to the restaurant. She was a little early but she wanted to check on Gino and see whether there had been any further developments.

Gino spotted Abby as soon as she came through the door, and escorted her to their best table. He scuttled away and came back with a glass of Prosecco which Abby gratefully took, giving him a big smile in return.

"So, how have you been Gino? Have you had any more problems with the police?" Abby asked.

"They tell me not to leave the island, but where would I go anyway?" he gesticulated with his hands, sweeping them in front of him as if pointing out the group of Balearic Islands that lay in front of him. "This is my home!" he said emphatically. "I don't want to leave this place."

"I don't think you have to Gino, I think it's just something they say. Until they have solved Mrs Cook's death I guess they just want to keep everyone together in one place to make it easier to find people." Abby tried to console him, offering the best explanation she could give in simple English.

"They don't believe me though!" Gino said, deflated.

"About what?" Abby asked gently.

"I tell them that day, I tell them, I see Mrs Cook with a gentleman, a younger gentleman, not the usual one."

MURDER IN MENORCA

Abby leaned closer. "What do you mean younger?" she asked excitedly. "And who is the usual one?"

Gino tried to explain that Mrs Cook, on her previous visits to the island, would often come in with an older gentlemen but on the night of her death he saw her with a different man, much younger than her usual companion.

"Did you tell the police about all this?" Abby asked.

"Of course, of course," Gino explained. "But the local police, they don't like me; they just think I make the story up."

"But why?" Abby asked, shocked that Gino's story had been so easily dismissed.

"It was only me here. Me, Mrs Cook and the young man. No-one else was here to say whether this was true or not."

"Even still!" Abby exclaimed. "Did you tell the English policeman?" Abby asked, sure James wouldn't have dismissed such an important line of investigation.

"No. But the other policemen write it down."

Abby patted Gino's hand affectionately. "Leave it with me, Gino, I will make sure someone looks into it for you." Abby said, confident she could tell James and he'd follow it up.

"Oh thank you Abby, thank you very much!" Gino gushed, kissing Abby on each cheek before running off toward Paolo, excitedly sharing his news.

Eveline and Jane arrived then and Abby shared what she had just learnt, wanting to know if the two ladies could shed any light on either of the men she'd heard about so far.

They chatted about what they had witnessed while spending time in Agnes Cook's company, trying to jog their memories, but failing to come up with anything until Jane took on a far-away look.

"Watch out," Eveline warned, "She's got something."

"How do you know?" Abby asked curiously.

"She's got that look. She always has that look when she's about to reveal something splendid."

"I think I remember…" started Jane.

"See!" interrupted Eveline excitedly.

Abby gave Eveline a stern look that she hoped said "Be quiet!" and given Eveline's response, she mimicked closing a zip across her mouth and throwing away the key, she thought it had worked a treat.

"Let me see," continued Jane, completely oblivious to the other two. "It was a few nights ago now, but I definitely remember Agnes arguing with a young man. I didn't think anything of it at the time though, just thought she was being her usual moaning self."

"Well now I wonder whether that could be the same man Gino saw Mrs Cook talking to the night she died," Abby thought out loud. "I don't suppose you remember what he looked like do you?"

MURDER IN MENORCA

"Hmmmm, I do remember being struck by his hair," Jane commented, moving her hand to her head and making some strange wavy shapes. "It was very grand, and very tall. It must have given him an extra 5 inches or so it was that tall!"

"Really!?" Eveline chimed in, "I wonder how he'd make it stand that tall!?"

"Kids can do anything these days," Jane explained wisely.

"So tall hair," Jane said, trying to bring the conversation back on track, "Anything else?"

"Well, I do remember thinking he was probably a bit old for such a wild haircut!" Jane giggled. "I mean he must have been older than you Abby, and you're no spring chicken are you dear?"

"Well speak for yourself!" Abby joked as she felt a little frisson of excitement inside. If she could match the description with Gino they could have a potential alternative suspect.

"Anything else?" Abby tried to tease any other details out of Jane.

"I don't think so dear. Other than that he was very ordinary looking. I'd say average height, black-brown hair, nothing unusual about his clothing or appearance other than the sticky-uppy hair, oh and he looked pasty white from afar, almost shining like a star in the dark, I thought that strange too. It emphasised his hair even more.

"So star-shiny skin and ridiculously tall hair, shouldn't be too hard to find hey ladies?" Abby summarised, to which Eveline started giggling.

"Star-shiny skin!?" she giggled, "I want some!" which made Jane break down into a fit of giggles too.

"Honestly," Jane chastised, "You two are like little kids sometimes!"

"Oh but that's how we keep ourselves so young," explained Eveline through the mad cackling.

Abby caught Paolo's eye, who came over to take the food order.

"Is Gino around? I want to ask him something," Abby asked excitedly, desperate to know whether Gino could describe the young man he'd seen with Mrs Cook.

"He'll be back in about 30 minutes, he's just gone to run an errand for me," Paolo explained, "Meanwhile ladies, what can I get you to eat?"

They ordered their food, Abby not sure whether she'd be able to eat it her stomach was turning so much in anticipation. If she could prove the two young men were one and the same surely that would get Gino off the hook and focus attention on this other man, whoever he was?

"You really must calm down dear," Eveline commented, noticing Abby's fidgeting hands.

"I can't, we could have a new suspect on our hands by the end of lunchtime," Abby enthused.

"Yes dear, but we also couldn't," Jane offered soberly.

"And even if we did, you can't tell Gino and get his hopes up as they'll only have so much further to travel down if they are then expelled," Eveline continued.

"And even if the descriptions do match, it could still mean nothing. There's nothing to say the police haven't ruled that whole line of questioning out already," Jane added.

"You two have spent far too long in each other's company!" Abby huffed.

"Maybe dear, but we're also right." said Jane.

"So settle those nerves and start thinking about your next move," advised Eveline.

"OK, tag team one, what are my next moves?"

"Easy dear. Firstly, you asked us about two gentleman, not one" Jane winked at Eveline who smiled broadly.

"Crap, you're right." Abby admitted, thinking maybe she did need to calm it down a bit. How did she miss asking about that? That was surely what they'd refer to as a rookie error in cop school. James would be so disappointed, Abby thought, smiling at the thought of him.

"Okay," Abby asked slowly, "we've covered the younger gentleman so now what about the older one? Any thoughts?"

"Oh yes dear, lots," they both chimed in together.

"Really?" Abby asked, surprised.

"Yes, that older man sounds like Mrs Cook's bit on the side." Jane confided.

"Her what!?" Abby spluttered.

"Agnes did not have a 'bit on the side' you silly old fool!" Evelined butted in. "He was Agnes's long lost love, so to speak."

"I don't get it," Abby looked from one woman to another, completely confused.

"As the story goes," Eveline explained, "Agnes came out here a long while ago, a few years after the death of her husband, and met the man she had almost married when younger."

"Oh it was such a romantic story," Jane took over, "They'd been separated from each other when younger and both had gone on to marry and have children. The man, George-something, I forget his full name, used to come out here every year, and it just so happened that one year, they bumped into each other, completely by accident, as fate would have it."

"And then they just kept on bumping into each other every year," Eveline rounded off the story. "It's rather sad really, and I don't know why they didn't just get together, I mean they were both widowed so there would have been no scandal in it."

"Maybe they had just gotten used to life on their own again," Jane suggested, "I mean can you imagine being saddled with another man at our age?"

Eveline shuddered, "Eurgh, I can think of nothing worse!" she grimaced.

Abby laughed, "You two want to watch out, you'll be getting reputations for yourselves speaking like that!"

"Dear, if I'd wanted another man around I would have gone out and got one, but they are altogether useless, and just get in the way. Besides, the only thing I can think of that they would be handy for is DIY, and I'd rather pay a younger, fitter one to come round and do that for me!" Eveline justified herself, all the while Jane nodding on encouraging.

"Quite!" Jane confirmed vigorously.

Abby laughed at them, wondering whether Mrs Cook had felt the same, and thinking about her own situation, and how she had started feeling the exact same after her marriage had ended so disappointingly. But then she thought of James, and all he had given her so far, and she was adamant that she hadn't given up on men quite yet, or at least not on one particular one.

With their lunch coming to an end, and Abby feeling like she had learnt lots more about Mrs Cook, she looked around for Gino, desperately wanting to corroborate his story, but he still hadn't returned from his errands.

"Do you fancy coming to the beach with us?" Eveline asked, "We're going paddle boarding."

"You're doing what!?" Abby asked incredulously.

"Paddle boarding, dear," Jane said a little louder, "It's the latest craze with all the youngsters," as if that explanation was enough.

"Yes, but that doesn't explain why you ladies are doing it?" Abby joked.

"It's massively fun!" Eveline explained.

"So my kids say," Abby admitted.

"Well there you go then, come on," Jane encouraged Abby.

I guess if they can do it, Abby thought. "Ok, I'll come," she said, feeling emboldened.

MURDER IN MENORCA

CHAPTER THIRTEEN

Not fully knowing what to expect, Abby was a little amused when they were met at the beach by a strapping 6 foot hunk of a man.

"Abby, meet Julio, our paddle board instructor" Jane smiled mischievously.

So this was why they'd looked so animated when talking about paddle boarding, Jane thought, rolling her eyes over the almost naked body of Julio, standing to attention in his tight red swim shorts.

"Julio," Eveline explained, "Abby would love to give paddle boarding a go, and we told her she simply had to have a lesson with you to learn the basics and get a real feel for the sport," Abby could almost hear Eveline purring, and was sure she was edging closer to the man, ready to pet him.

"Abby, darling!" Julio started with a Birmingham accent.

Abby almost burst out laughing at Julio's voice, guessing he was actually a Julian. She had definitely not expected the man to be from the Midlands with a body as tanned as his was, but the other two seemed not to mind one iota, hanging off his every word as he ran through the safety procedure before getting each of the ladies a board.

"Right ladies, let's get out there!" Julio shouted encouragingly.

Balancing on the board was easier than Abby had expected, though she was a little bit disappointed to discover that the paddle board had been built to be easier to stay on. The added benefit of a snug lifejacket made her feel much more secure about going so far out onto the water.

They spent almost 2 hours out on the water. Abby was bowled over by the beauty of the coves and the stillness of the sea, almost being lulled into a meditative state by the tranquillity of it all. She wasn't though, as she was regularly brought back to the present by Eveline and Jane who flipped between laughing and bickering with each other about what adventure they were going to embark on next. Julio seemed to find the whole thing wildly amusing and when Abby wasn't laughing at Eveline and Jane's cackling laughter she found herself giggling at Julio's hooting laugh. He was a fantastic teacher though, talking them through different techniques and telling them about the land around which they travelled.

To Abby's complete surprise she absolutely loved paddle boarding and jumped back onto land with a disappointing jolt. She didn't see James watching from the beachfront bar as she hugged Julio, thanking him for an amazing experience, didn't notice him as she walked back up the sand with Eveline and Jane, chatting about what a fun experience paddle boarding had been, and didn't catch him hide behind a menu as they strolled past the bar towards the hotel.

Abby couldn't wait to tell her boys she had tried their new favourite sport. She hoped they'd be impressed, but expected they'd just be embarrassed, as was the teenage way with everything.

She decided to give James a call as she reached her room, finding herself wanting to share her amazing experience with him, but his phone went to answer machine so she left a message.

James was far too busy berating himself at the bar still, annoyed at how jealous he'd been seeing Abby hugging another man. It had been obvious that she was just thanking the instructor but the feelings of jealousy that gurgled in his stomach reminded him of how he'd felt when he'd discovered his ex-wife had cheated on him with his best friend. Did he really want to get close enough to another woman and open himself up to that level of hurt again?

Even as he acknowledged his own stupidity, James couldn't help but revel in it, allowing himself to wallow in self-pity for a while before sending himself home for being ridiculous.

CAT PRESTON

CHAPTER FOURTEEN

At breakfast the next morning Abby revealed her new found spirited side to her boys, who were flabbergasted that she'd actually tried something new.

"Nice one, Mum" Luke said, "Maybe you could come out with us one day if you like?"

"Yeah, you can show off your moves," Will agreed.

Abby beamed, feeling bad for thinking they'd just be embarrassed of her.

"How are you feeling this morning dear?" Jane approached, her hand lying awkwardly on her hip.

"Great!" Abby said, "But you don't look too great? Are you okay?"

"Oh yes dear," Jane smiled, "Just old age trying to get the best of me. So what are you three up to today?"

"We're heading into Mahon this morning," Abby shared.

"We have to run over to the restaurant first though Mum, I left my coat there last night," Will piped up.

"Okay, so we're heading over to the restaurant and then going into Mahon" Abby affirmed.

"Be sure to try out the glass bottom boat trip won't you, it's fab," Jane suggested, "And before you leave, have a word with Mr Nugent over there," Jane added, pointing to a middle-aged man in tortoiseshell spectacles reading the paper. "Eveline was chatting to him this morning and he also remembers that young man we were talking about yesterday".

"Oh great, will do," Abby thanked Jane before asking, "Where's your partner-in-crime this morning Jane?"

Jane laughed, "She pulled a muscle last night so is seeing the doctor about some pain medication the silly old bat!"

As Jane wandered off Will turned to Abby and said "I can't believe them two went paddle boarding!"

"I know!" Luke agreed.

"Well let's hope we're all doing stuff like that when we get to that age! It's pretty cool really" Will added, surprising Abby who had to date only heard stereotypical comments coming out of her son's mouths about Eveline and Jane. She leaned over and ruffled Will's hair, who pushed her away with the standard "Mum!!"

While the boys helped themselves to more pastries, stocking up on food before their road trip to Mahon – a total of 30 minutes on a bus – Abby made her way over to the other side of the restaurant to speak with Mr Nugent.

He peered over his paper as she approached, realised who it was and folded the paper with a big smile, "Abby!" he exclaimed, "I haven't seen you around for a day or two!" he greeted her warmly.

Mr Nugent had arrived with his family, his wife and 4 girls, the same day Abby and her boys had arrived, and this was the first time Abby had noticed him without one of his girls hanging off of him.

"Where are all your beautiful girls?" Abby asked.

Mr Nugent winked, "I'm getting a sneaky bit of me-time. I treated the missus and daughters to a manicure at the spa, all rather selfishly of course, but they weren't about to pass up on the offer just so I could get a quiet 30 minutes with my paper."

"A-ha!" Abby grinned, "Good move!"

"I thought so!" he agreed. "So Eveline was saying you would want to know about the man I saw with Mrs Cook?" Mr Nugent got right to the point, wanting to get back to his paper.

"Yes, I was just wondering if you could tell me when you saw them and whether you could describe him to me?" Abby asked.

"It was the night after we arrived actually," Mr Nugent revealed. "We'd just had a delicious Greek meal at the Acropolis and we were wandering back to the hotel when the girls spotted the café on the front with the inflatables and amusement games. The wife agreed to take them down while I had a sneaky cigar up top. I saw him following Mrs Cook back from the main part of town. She looked anxious to get away from him, like he was harassing her about something, but she seemed to know him, from how she acted anyway. I offered to walk her back to her room and he backed off immediately, almost shying away as if he didn't want to be recognised."

"And would you recognise him again?" Abby asked hopefully.

"Oh without a doubt" Mr Nugent nodded, "What with that ghastly haircut. What kind of man wears his hair like that at our age, he can't have been much younger than me, if he was at all!"

"Can you describe him to me?" Abby coaxed.

"Well now, let me see, he was an average looking chap, except for the frightful hair of course. Wore it standing up on end, god knows how much hair product he needed to carry off that ridiculous style. Something you would expect of a 17 year old maybe, but not a fully grown man for heaven's sake!" Mr Nugent scoffed.

"And you didn't notice any other redeeming features, Mr Nugent?"

"Not really, as I said, a fairly average looking chap. Maybe 5'10", 5'11", dressed like a teenager with tight jeans and flamboyant shirt, but other than that, nothing really that stood out I'm afraid."

"Well thanks so much for that," Abby said gratefully.

"I hope it helps," Mr Nugent said warmly. "Though I did tell the English policeman about him so I suspect they have it in hand."

"Detective McEwan?" Abby checked.

"Yes, that's him, nice chap," Mr Nugent confirmed.

Abby's heart sank a bit at that news. She was hoping to surprise James with the news that she had single-handedly found a potentially new suspect, to make up for being embarrassed about going on about the cleaner being someone he should look into, which turned into a complete dead-end. Now all she would be doing is corroborating a story.

Maybe if she tagged along to the restaurant with the boys before their big road trip she could get Gino to confirm that was the same young man that he had seen.

When the boys had finished stuffing their faces with pastries and Abby had downed another cup of coffee they headed over to the restaurant. While Luke found his coat Abby made a beeline for Gino, who she found behind the bar, cutting up lemons.

"Remember telling me that you saw Mrs Cook with a younger man the night of her death?" Abby asked, getting straight to the point.

"Yes," Gino answered hesitantly.

"Can you describe him to me?" Abby had her fingers crossed behind her back, compelling Gino to describe the same man who had now been described to her by two separate individuals.

"I can't remember," Gino hesitated.

"Try!" Abby pushed a bit too harshly. "It's important that you try to remember. It might be extremely important information."

Gino looked at Abby blankly for what felt like the longest time, and then said "He had black hair."

"Yes..." Abby prompted. "What else?"

"He was wearing a very big shirt, lots of colour. Loud, yes?" Gino said, unsure of himself.

"Okay," Abby encouraged, "That's good. Anything more you can think of? Anything at all?"

"Oh he wear lots of perfume. Very strong. Made me cough." Gino added, before drifting into some type of daydream.

Abby left him alone for a minute, turning back to her boys who were both standing at the door.

"We'll miss the bus," Luke mouthed, pointing to his wristwatch.

Abby turned back to Gino, almost willing him to add something, anything.

"His hair was funny," he finally said.

"Yes!" Abby couldn't help herself. "What was funny about his hair?" she tried again, trying to maintain a more professional edge.

"Very ...up?" Gino tried, using his hand to demonstrate what he meant, and holding it a few inches above his head.

Abby smiled. "Okay, Gino, I think I've got what I need. I'm going to have a word with the police as I think this man should be investigated properly."

Gino looked confused, but Paolo, who had been standing to the side, listening in, came round to the front of the bar and gave Abby a great, big bear hug.

"Thank you," Paolo said, "And thank you for believing him!"

"Mum!" Will called, trying to hurry the conversation along for fear of missing the bus.

Abby started to move towards the door, Gino still confused about what had just been said, but Paolo waved them off, calling after them, "I'll explain to Gino, and thank you again".

"I haven't done anything!" Abby warned, "I'm just going to ask that they ensure they look into this other man. It may yet not mean anything."

"It means something," Paolo seemed convinced.

MURDER IN MENORCA

CHAPTER FIFTEEN

The boys almost dragged Abby out of the door, and they made a run for it as they saw the bus pull up halfway up the road, Abby trying to keep up with them but failing miserably.

Luke reached the bus first and kept it waiting until Abby caught up. As she clambered on board, sweat dripping down her back and her lungs feeling like they were about to explode, she collapsed into the front seat, panting away as if she had just completed a marathon.

"Jeez, Mum, you really need to exercise more," Will said, shocked at how unfit his mum was.

"I know," Abby puffed, "I've never been good at running."

They settled in for the 30 minute bus ride, which gave Luke more than enough time to ask about Gino and what it all meant.

"I'm not sure yet," Abby explained, "but apparently when Gino was interviewed by the local police they completely dismissed his story about the young man he'd seen with Mrs Cook. The fact that both Jane and Mr Nugent also seen an altercation between Mrs Cook and a man who they all described the same, can't be a coincidence."

"But don't the police know about this?" asked Will.

"I'm not sure what they know," Abby admitted. "But I know that they don't know Jane's story as she'd completely forgotten about the incident until Eveline and I jogged her memory. And if the local police dismissed Gino's story, I'm not sure whether they'd have told James or not."

"James?" Luke and Will both chimed in together.

"Who's James, Mum?" asked Will.

"Detective McEwan," Abby said, realising she was about to get rumbled.

"And so how long has Detective McEwan been just 'James'?" Luke asked, trying the whole innocent act but failing miserably due to the huge grin spreading across his face.

"Oh shush you two!" Abby nudged Will, who was sitting next to her, and gave some appropriately evil eye glares at her eldest, sitting across from them.

"Mum's got a boyfriend, Mum's got a boyfriend," Will started singing softly.

"Will!" Abby warned, "I have not! We've had lunch that's all. Jeez!"

Will and Luke shared a knowing look between them before placating Abby with an "Alright Mum, it was just lunch. We believe you!"

Abby sat silently in her seat, squirming with embarrassment, for a few minutes before trying to change the subject.

"I could do with another coffee already. Who wants to stop off at a café before we go to the market?"

"Me!" Will nodded. "I'm desperate for the loo!"

"Honestly!" Abby rolled her eyes, wondering what age kids got to before they stopped needing the toilet as soon as they'd left the house. She was pretty sure Will did it just to wind her up sometimes as he made such a habit of it.

Mahon was beautiful, full of lovely little old streets with gorgeously intricate old buildings. Abby could have wandered around the cobbled alleyways for the whole day, but the boys had one thing on their minds and she wouldn't get any peace until they'd grabbed the shoes they'd set out for.

As they both tried on the Menorcan sandals Abby looked unconvinced, "Aren't they a bit unisex for you two?" she asked, noting that both men and women seemed to be wearing this particular shoe everywhere they went.

"No Mum, that's the point of them. Everyone wears them here. We can't leave without buying some. It just wouldn't be right!" Luke explained.

"Yeah," Will backed up his brother. "You can get some too if you want."

"Oh that's kind of you, Will," Abby said, knowing full well that she'd be the one paying for all these shoes.

They were nice though, Abby conceded, as she checked out a pair of rainbow-inspired ones, with reds and greens and yellows amongst the cream base.

The boys choices were much more sedate, Luke taking the dark blue ones and Will opting for the dark green colour.

With everyone sorted on the shoe front, they decided to hunt out a restaurant for lunch before heading over to the marina and doing the glass bottomed boat tour.

Abby was pleasantly surprised by the boat tour, marvelling at the remains of the old naval hospital and the old Mola fort. Abby hadn't realised the island was draped in so much history and was fascinated by the architecture on the tour. The boys meanwhile spent most of the time underground, hunting down the colourful fish swimming past, and whiling away the time holding a contest over who could spot the biggest eel.

MURDER IN MENORCA

CHAPTER SIXTEEN

They got back to the bus station with 5 minutes to spare and joined the long queue of people waiting to get a ride back to Arenal. The boys had managed to coax Abby into buying them a couple of t-shirts too, and she'd even been persuaded to buy herself a pretty, emerald green summer dress which went perfectly with her new shoes. Abby felt extremely pleased with herself as she settled back into a seat on the bus. She'd had a lovely day with her boys, some delicious food, and an amazing trip on the glass bottom boat and had even got herself a brand spanking new outfit. All in all, a most successful day, she thought happily.

As the bus pulled away from the station Abby's eyes closed over, ready for a well-deserved nap. She was rudely awoken only minutes later by Will, who was tugging on her top.

"Mum," Will whispered, "Don't look now but you know that man we were talking about earlier, I think he's sitting 2 rows behind us."

Abby's eyes shot open and she had to stop herself from turning round and finding out whether the potential suspect was sitting only yards away from them. She managed to wait a few moments before turning around slowly and looking over her shoulder.

Abby noticed it immediately, the tall, spikey hair.

"Oh my god," she whispered to Will. Will nudged Luke, who was sitting in the seats next to theirs, across the aisle.

"What?" Luke moaned, half-opening one eye.

Will mouthed a message about the guy two seats back, which made Luke turn and look. The look on his face told Abby everything she needed to know.

They were sitting on the bus with the potential suspect in Mrs Cook's murder. She grabbed her phone out of her bag and tried to call James, but there was no signal on the bus.

"Drat!" she complained. "No signal."

"Who were you going to phone?" Will asked.

"James," Abby answered automatically before realising she was about to get stick again.

Will leaned over to Luke, "Mum's trying James," he smirked.

"Will you two behave!" Abby hissed. "This is serious!"

Abby kept her phone in her hand until she noticed 2 bars on her phone, and immediately dialled James's number, but he wasn't answering.

"Now what?" Abby asked, wondering how to play this. She didn't want to lose the man now that she had found him, but she certainly didn't want to put herself in a situation where he could identify her, or more importantly, her sons.

"We could follow him?" suggested Luke.

"No way!" Abby said, not at all happy with that suggestion.

"From a distance Mum, we're not going to walk right up behind him. We'll hang right back, just to see where he's staying." Luke persisted.

"Then we can call your man, James." Will added. "I've followed people before, it's pretty easy. Plus, I love Spooks so I've got the technique right down."

"Why on earth have you been following people?" Abby asked, more than a little concerned about the extracurricular activities of her youngest son.

"Don't worry, Mum, if we find ourselves in any danger we can always call James, right Will?" Luke smirked.

"Oh yeah, cos he's gonna answer his phone on the first ring, just like he did right now." Abby answered sarcastically.

They were still arguing about whether to follow him or not when they reached their stop. Abby stood, "Come on!" she ordered her boys.

As she pulled Will up she noticed the sticky-up hair guy had also stood.

"Oh no," said Abby, motioning to Luke with her eyes.

He caught her movement and looked in the direction she was motioning towards, noticing the man and standing up, dragging Will with him.

All three of them disembarked from the bus and stood stock still, waiting for the man, who was a mere two steps ahead of them, to move on. Thankfully he didn't seem to notice them and started sauntering up the road.

"Right, let's hold on until he's a fair way away and then we'll follow behind," Luke suggested.

"We could do a Spooks style follow and take it in turns, using our phones," Will said, checking the GPS on his phone was working and getting altogether far too excited about the prospect for Abby.

"Can we just hold on one minute!" Abby said, exasperated. "We are talking about following a potential killer!" she explained. "You two are all I have and I am in no way putting either of you in danger," she finished, folding her arms and nodding her head, confident in her decision.

The boys just looked at her, Luke rolling her eyes and Will tutting his disapproval.

"Honestly Mum," Will moaned, "You're so old-fashioned sometimes!"

"Ha!" Abby guffawed. "I'd rather be old-fashioned than a reckless mother."

"Mum, you are being slightly ridiculous." Luke scolded. "It's not like we're going to take a run at him and tackle him to the ground."

"I don't care!" Abby insisted, noticing that her legs were moving in unison with her those of both sons, in the direction the mysterious man had headed off in.

"Oi!" Abby nudged Luke. She grabbed Will's upper arm, forcing him to stop. "We're not doing this."

"Do you want to help Gino or not?" Luke asked, using guilt to try to make Abby come round to his way of thinking.

He could tell from her momentary hesitation that it had worked somewhat. "This is as close as we get," she warned.

Luke and Will high-fived, and now it was Abby's turn to do some eye rolling.

The mystery man was quite a far way ahead at this point so they had to hustle to keep him within eyeshot.

Abby was impressed with the way her boys kept their distance and worked as a team, even going so far as to suggest they could both open up a private detective agency, in jest of course. They both took the suggestion a lot more seriously than she'd meant it to be though, and started planning what kind of clients they would have.

As they approached one of the resort hotels Abby lay a steadying hand on each of her boys, holding them back while she assessed whether the mystery man was going to go into the hotel or not. They watched from across the road, ducking behind a parked car, as the man made his way through a little passageway and appeared seconds later walking along the first floor balcony. He fumbled in his pocket for a minute before pausing at one of the hotel room doors, putting the key in the lock and closing the door behind him.

"Okay," Abby said cautiously, "We've got him."

"Shall we hang around and see if he comes back out again?" Will asked.

"Why?" Abby asked, "There's no point. We know where he is now. We can report it to the police."

"Can you read the door number?" Luke asked, squinting at the number plate next to the hotel room door.

Abby squinted but couldn't make it out. "I can describe it," she decided.

"Yeah but they're gonna want the number," Luke said.

"I could run over the road," Will suggested.

"Absolutely not." Abby stated, clutching Will's arm in case he tried to make a dart for it.

Luke edge a little bit closer to the road, and then nonchalantly crossed over, before heading off down the road, in the opposite direction from where they had come. Abby and Will followed his lead, keeping to their side of the road.

When they were sure they were out of sight of the hotel room, Abby grabbed Will and crossed over.

"It's Room 297," Luke said softly.

"Okay, good work boys. Now let's get back to Paolo's and I'll buy you both a drink to calm your nerves. I could certainly do with one!" Abby exhaled slowly, not realising she had been holding her breath.

On the way back to the restaurant Abby tried James again, realising she hadn't spoken to him in what felt like forever but was actually a little more than a day. Where was he anyway? She missed him, and wanted desperately to share her news, but she'd already left a couple of voicemails and at this point she was in danger of coming off as desperate.

She decided to wait for the morning, if he didn't want to talk to her then that was his choice. If she didn't see him the next morning she would go to the local police station and fill them in on what she'd learnt instead.

Paolo had obviously had some good news, as they were having a small celebratory party at his restaurant. Paolo embraced Abby as soon as he saw her, "Thank you!" he proclaimed.

Abby blushed, not at all sure what she was being thanked for, until Paolo explained James had been in to the restaurant and had questioned Gino fully, promising to investigate the presence of the mystery man.

It was this news that Paolo and his family were celebrating and Abby and the boys were invited to join the family for a typical Spanish meal, which meant drinking copious amounts of Spanish wine, or at least it did for Abby. Luke managed a couple of beers and Will was limited to one due to his age, not that Abby was under any illusion that he wouldn't have tried more with his friends, but it wasn't something that she was going to condone.

James had listened to Abby's message that day, feeling remorse at his behaviour the night before and stupid for missing out on seeing her. He kicked himself when he learnt she had spoken with Gino and had identified a potential witness, someone he had come across when interviewing one

111

of the hotel guests, but who he hadn't yet followed up on fully due to other lines of enquiry.

James had hot-footed it over to Paolo's restaurant and missed Abby and the boys by mere minutes. He had managed to corroborate the appearance of the additional suspect, and had gone straight back to the police station to try to learn more about the mystery man, and more importantly, find out why none of the local police had cared to mention the man.

Busy following up leads back home, James had missed the second call by Abby and had vowed to follow it up in person the next morning, surprising Abby with breakfast.

MURDER IN MENORCA

CHAPTER SEVENTEEN

Abby woke up the next morning with a banging red wine headache. She dragged herself out of bed and into the kitchenette to get some bottled water out of the fridge before tiptoeing back to her room, not wanting to wake the boys.

"You alright, Mum?" Luke asked, casually walking out of his room as if he didn't have a care in the world.

"Feeling delicate," Abby whispered, her hand on the door knob, anxious to get back to bed.

Abby looked Luke up and down, confused, "How come you're so perky this time in the morning?" she asked.

"I'm not sure really," Luke muttered, "I barely drank anything, unlike you! Oh, and I met a girl."

"Another one?" Abby blurted out.

"This one's different Mum," Luke explained.

"Hmmmm," Abby wasn't so convinced. "Aren't they all!" she called out as she escaped into her room and collapsed face first onto the bed.

She must have fallen asleep within seconds as she woke up with a start some time later, her head banging like a drum, before realising it wasn't her head at all, but the door.

113

Wearing nothing but her cosy M&S pyjamas Abby made her way to the door. She heaved it open with a heavy breath, before it caught in her throat at the sight of James and she very unceremoniously broke into a fit of coughing before she could even say hello.

"You look awful!" James said, barely containing a laugh that threatened to explode from his throat.

Abby grumbled something incoherent and pushed the door open, moving back into the room and collapsing on the couch.

"Where are the boys?" James asked.

"I have no idea!" Abby admitted. "Luke was awake at some ungodly hour this morning, all happy over a girl he met, and Will's probably still in bed."

"Do you want a cup of tea?" asked James, taking pity on the pathetic sight in front of him.

"Oh, I'd love a cup of tea!" Abby exclaimed, before grabbing the blanket draped over the couch and wrapping herself in it.

While James busied himself in the kitchenette making tea and toast Abby switched the tv on and zoned out to an old movie she'd seen a million times before.

James brought over the tea and toast on a little tray and laid them on the coffee table. Abby shuffled to one side to make space for James to sit on the couch and thankfully grabbed the toast he offered.

"So, what were you upto last night?" James asked.

"We were at Paolo's," Abby explained, in between mouthfuls of toast. "You heard my message," she beamed at him then, and he couldn't help but lean over and kiss her quickly on the lips.

Abby moved away, "Don't kiss me!" she stammered, wiping her face to check she hadn't left a load of toast crumbs on it. "I'm a mess!" she explained.

James merely chuckled. "I've seen worse," he laughed. "So how much did you drink?"

"I don't know. Three glasses of red wine, maybe even four," Abby moaned.

"Well that's not that much!" James said, encouragingly.

"I know. But I can't handle alcohol. Anything more than one glass and I'm anyone's," Abby said, before her eyes shot up to meet James and she quickly stammered, "I don't mean that!"

James just laughed playfully. "Shall I tell you a secret to make you feel better?" he asked.

"Yes," Abby whispered.

"I saw you paddle boarding," James confessed.

"Did you? Why didn't you come and say hi?" Abby felt a little bit proud of the fact that he'd seen her doing something she now considered cool.

"Promise you won't laugh?" James asked.

Abby nodded her head cautiously, wondering what on earth he'd seen. Surely she'd not been so bad as to make him run?

"I saw you with the instructor," he started.

"Yes..." Abby prompted.

"Hugging him..." James words trailed off.

Abby looked up at him, completely confused. "Yes? I don't get it?"

"I stomped off in a jealous huff!" James finally admitted, looking any which way but directly into Abby's eyes, which was incredibly hard to do. Abby looked at him, confusion turning to shock turning to incredulity.

"You thought what? I was going to try and rip his pants off?" Abby tried keeping a straight face but a smile was working its way into her put-on frown so much it was making her cheek muscles ache. She finally gave in and gave James the biggest smile she could muster in her delicate state.

"You were jealous?" she asked, still grinning away.

"I was jealous," James admitted.

"I love that!" Abby admitted, her head resting back onto the couch.

"You love that I was jealous?" James asked, confused. If anything he'd thought she'd be completely turned off by his childish paddy.

"No, that's just ridiculous!" Abby confirmed his thoughts. "I love that you had to tell me."

MURDER IN MENORCA

It was James's turn now for his emotions to play out on his face, as Abby watched his confusion turn his eyebrows inwards and his easy smile into a frown.

"I'm confused," James said, watching Abby as she lay on the couch with a small smile playing on his lips.

"I can see that!" Abby grinned, feeling much better after toast. She swigged down her cup of tea and stood, her hand reaching up to her head so her fingertips could massage her temple.

"Aspirin?" James asked.

"Please," Abby smiled guiltily, motioning to the cupboard above the sink, where she had put the holiday first aid kit. She winced slightly as her senses started to return to normal and she realised she was standing in front of James in her worn pyjamas. Before she could do anything about her own disastrous wardrobe, an even bigger disaster made his way out of the bedroom door.

"Mum!" Will exclaimed, firstly noticing James, and then his Mum. Abby winced as he took on the role of "man-of-the-house", standing before them looking suspiciously at James.

Abby's mouth opened but nothing came out. Her son on the other hand had no such problem.

"So this is James!" Will started. "Has he been here all night?"

"And what if he has?" Abby asked, not at all impressed that she was being read the riot act by her 15 year old.

"I haven't," James tried to interject.

117

CAT PRESTON

Abby shushed him and Will just gave him a stony glare, obviously not happy that his Mum was parading around the room in her pyjamas with a strange man around.

Will didn't know what to do next. He'd come out of the bedroom and almost jumped at the sight of the policeman he recognised from around the hotel, and then his Mum looking ridiculous in her pyjamas. He'd immediately decided to go for playing it hard, wanting to see his Mum squirm, but it wasn't quite working out the way he'd intended it to, and now he was simply looking for an escape. Will's escape came with the very timely opening of the apartment door.

"Well, well, what do we have here?" Luke smirked as he walked into the apartment, his eyes darting from his little brother to his Mum and her who-knew-what.

Abby groaned, and watched as James tried to make himself invisible by sidling up to the wall separating the kitchenette from the entranceway. She didn't envy him, facing up to two over-protective teenage boys.

James decided to go down the safe route and play the police card. He knew it'd come in handy at some point.

"Relax boys," he tried, "Your Mum and I were just discussing Mrs Cook's murder."

"Oh!" Will said, looking dejected at the fact that the fun of teasing his Mum was over before it had even began.

Abby heaved a sigh of relief before scrunching up her nose and wincing even harder than before at Luke's next words.

"So you told him about our adventure yesterday then?"

"What adventure?" James asked, caution creeping into his voice.

"Oooooo," Will said, "You didn't tell him, did you?"

Abby was sure he was trying to make things worse.

"Boys," she demanded, "Go to your room!" she said in her best commanding voice, holding her head and she shouted.

Luke and Will sniggered as they closed the door to their room, and she could clearly hear them insinuating that Abby was now going to be in trouble with the cops.

James stood in the middle of the living room now, one eyebrow cocked, waiting for the explanation of whatever it was that had got them all in a tizz.

"Can I get dressed first?" Abby asked, playing for time, knowing James wasn't going to be happy about her antics.

"Do you honestly need to?" James asked, starting to get a bad feeling about Abby's resistance to telling him what was going on.

Abby tried pleading with her eyes, really not wanting to get shouted at like a naughty teenager practically in front of her own teenagers.

"Fine!" James relented. "Go, but be quick about it!"

Ten minutes later Abby reappeared in the living room, looking much more presentable in shorts and t-shirt. She slipped her feet into her flip flops and motioned for the door.

"It's that bad?" James queried.

"If you're going to shout I really don't want you doing it in front of my kids." Abby explained, walking out of the apartment door and looking behind her as she went, to make sure James was following.

A mixture of intrigue and panic found itself weaving a path into James's stomach. What could be so bad as to warrant being out of earshot of her kids? James wondered.

By the time she was partway through telling him about following the mystery man from the bus stop, James held his hand up, stopping Abby in full flow.

"I honestly don't want to hear any more," he said. "I just, how could you be so irresponsible? Why didn't you phone me?"

"I did," Abby stuttered, defensively.

"And why didn't you phone the local police?" James persisted.

"I don't know their number," Abby explained.

"And you didn't just think to turn away and report it when you got back to your room?" James critiqued.

"Report what?" Abby shot back. "Oh, I saw a guy who looked like someone that someone else described to me. What good would that have done me?"

James couldn't argue with that logic, and the fact that they now had somewhere to look was a big deal, but he wasn't about to give Abby any credit for putting herself and her boys in potential danger.

"What if he had noticed you?" James tried.

"I know. We kept far back," Abby admitted.

"You couldn't have kept that far back if you got a hotel room number, could you?" James didn't even want to think about what could have happened if the man had become suspicious and realised he was being followed.

"How do you even know he didn't notice you and lead you down the garden path? Or follow you home?" James continued.

"Alright," Abby shouted, having had enough of being berated about something she knew she'd been stupid to do. "I get it, okay? I get that it was stupid and reckless. But I thought I was being helpful."

"Yes, it was stupid!" James warned, getting more furious with every scenario he imagined entering his head.

"Oh for god's sake!" Abby cried, exasperated. "I'm a grown woman James. I am more than capable of making my own decisions thank you very much. And if I want to follow someone at a more than appropriately safe distance then I will."

"Well I better not catch you doing it Abby," James shouted back, "Or I'll have you arrested."

"For what?" Abby argued.

"A many number of things," James shot back. "Chief amongst them being the endangering of minors!" regretting saying it as soon as it left his mouth. But he was too late.

Abby felt like she'd been sucker punched, the breath flew out of her so fast she felt herself sway. Had she really endangered her own children? Had she really done something that horrific? The look on her face as she turned and walked away would stay with James for a long time.

He struggled with the notion of running after her, apologising for hitting her exactly where he knew it would hurt her the most, but the policeman side of him wanted to go and check out the last known location of the potential suspect, and it was this side that won out in the end.

Abby walked down the path toward the beach utterly dejected, feeling guiltier than she had in a long time. She hadn't felt threatened at all during their little escapade yesterday, always making sure her and her boys kept a more than reasonable distance from the mystery man. But maybe her logic had been flawed? She had no reason to follow the man, and no reason whatsoever to potentially endanger her boys. Feeling completely shaken up, Abby felt tears threaten to spill over onto her cheeks.

"Abby!" she heard, turning round at the familiar voice.

It was Eveline, waving at her from one of the hotel balconies. Abby waved back half-heartedly, not really wanting to talk to anyone.

"Come up Abby, we have someone to introduce you to!" Eveline persisted.

"Can I catch up with you some other time?" Abby shouted back, "I'm not feeling too good."

"No!" Eveline shouted back adamantly.

Abby sighed, "Fine, I'll be there in a minute."

Knocking on Eveline's hotel room door, Abby tried to pull herself together, but when Jane answered the door and pulled her into a wonderfully comforting hug Abby felt a tear trickle down her cheek, and a sob escape her throat.

"We saw what happened dear," Jane explained. "Are you okay?"

"I just feel so stupid," Abby explained, wiping her moist cheeks. .

"Don't be silly dear, he was dreadful, just dreadful," Jane patted Abby's back, before pulling her through the door.

Eveline was sitting out on the balcony with another older lady, chatting animatedly.

"Who's that?" Abby asked, not really in the mood for being chatty.

"We have a new development in the case," Jane whispered, conspiratorially.

"Oh no!" Abby warned. "I've had enough of involving myself in places I'm not wanted."

"Nonsense, dear!" Jane scolded, waving her hand as if brushing off some unwanted attention. "Don't let that old misery guts put you off your game."

Eveline came in from the balcony just then, wondering what was taking them so long. Seeing Jane's tear-stained cheeks she simply commented, "Forget the idiot! He's a man, what did you expect! Thinking they are the only ones who can protect others, the bloody cheek!"

"She's right you know dear," Jane agreed, "If at any time you would have felt like your boys were actually in danger, do you honestly think you wouldn't have gotten them out of the situation straightaway?"

"Well, I shouldn't have put them in the situation in the first place," Abby acknowledged.

"Abby, your boys are not little. In our day they would have been packed off to war. You can't molly coddle them all their lives," Jane scolded.

Eveline motioned to the lady still sitting on the balcony, "Pull yourself together Abigail! We've got work to do." And with that, Abby was lead outside, where tea and cake were waiting. What couldn't be fixed with tea and cake, Abby thought.

MURDER IN MENORCA

CHAPTER EIGHTEEN

When everyone was seated around the ornate little table and the tea had been poured Eveline lay her hand on the lady's wrist.

"Tell Abigail what you told us Miss Cherry." Before interrupting herself, "We met Miss Cherry on a bus trip yesterday. We got chatting and realised we both knew Mrs Cook, but Miss Cherry knows her from her previous visits, and has some rather interesting and pertinent information about our mutual friend."

"So sad to hear the news," Miss Cherry started, "But of course I wasn't shocked to hear about Agnes's death, what with her being so ill and all."

Abby's ears perked up, "Really?" she asked, her interest piqued in spite of herself.

"Yes, she'd been ill for years." Miss Cherry confirmed. "I think her son was the cause of most of her stress, he was forever after her for her money and what not."

Once Miss Cherry started talking it was hard to get a word in edgeways, so Abby, Eveline and Jane just sat listening, finishing off most of the cake and all of the tea. Jane even went back into the room to make more tea, and by the time she came back out again Miss Cherry was still warbling on about Mrs Cook.

125

There was so much inane information that it was hard to keep abreast of the real nuggets. Abby wanted desperately to get out her notebook and start scribbling details, but she'd left her handbag inside the apartment and didn't want to go back in to retrieve it in case she missed another nugget.

The ladies learnt that Mrs Cook had an ongoing feud with her one and only son, who by all account was a bit of a miscreant, being involved in various petty misdemeanours and constantly owing money to loan sharks and betting shops.

Mrs Cook had apparently had enough after one rather large debt she'd had to pay off, and had decided to cut her son off, to try to frighten him into shaping up. The year before last Miss Cherry remembered several conversations about whether or not to write him out of her will even.

Abby was buzzing with excitement by the time Miss Cherry finally ran out of breath. Forgetting all her feelings of inadequacy from her earlier conversation with James, she thanked Eveline and Jane profusely before tearing out of the apartment to try to find James and fill him in on the latest development.

Abby almost ran back down the path and towards the hotel reception, bumping into James as she skirted round the corner.

"Oh!" she exclaimed, shocked at having found him so fast.

"I've been looking for you," James said, his heart heavy with regret at how he had spoken to Abby earlier.

"Did you go to the other hotel?" Abby asked anxiously.

"Yes," James confirmed. "He wasn't there. I've left a constable on watch over there. As soon as he shows up we'll nab him."

Abby opened her mouth to speak but James cut her off by placing his finger on her lips and speaking before she had a second to protest.

"Please just let me speak first," he said, pleading with her.

Abby kept silent, desperate to share her news but also wanting to know what James had to say, hoping it was to admit he was a big oaf earlier.

"I'm so sorry about what I said earlier," he started.

"So you should be," Abby couldn't help but interject.

"It was a horrible thing to say, and I honestly, as soon as the words came out of my mouth I wanted to shove them back in."

Abby looked at him in stony silence, momentarily forgetting her own news as she remembered how awful James had made her feel about her mothering skills.

She wanted to say something, but suddenly found that she couldn't as she knew her voice would break and she'd get teary if she did, and she absolutely did not want to do that. So instead she stood, waiting for more.

James looked at Abby, noticing her eyes misting up and realising he'd hurt her even more than he'd originally allowed himself to acknowledge. It felt like a dagger through his chest to see the hurt shining in her eyes so much, and knowing that he was the cause of her pain.

What words could take back what had already been spoken?

"Abby," he started, unsure of how to finish, and deciding to just go with the truth. "You're an amazing mother. Those boys dote on you, it's obvious, and you don't get that level of love from being a bad parent. I was just being a dick. And I was scared."

"Scared?" Abby scoffed. "Of what?"

"Of what could have happened if something had gone wrong," he conceded. "Of what could have happened to you if something had gone wrong."

Bloody man, Abby thought. She almost wanted him to say something mean just so she could use a bit of anger to control the emotion that was threatening to pour out of her. You absolutely better not cry, Abby scolded herself.

"I just," James continued, unaware of the inner turmoil tearing Abby up, "I've seen things that's all, seen how badly things that we thought were under our control can go very badly wrong." He was mumbling now, not wanting to say the words that were trying to make their way out. It was way too early for those words to be said.

Okay, I can deal with this level of discussion, Abby thought, hoping it didn't start getting too personal again.

"I'm falling for you," James blurted out, not able to help himself.

"What?" Abby gasped, confusion written all over her face. "You're what?" She hadn't heard words like that in so long she didn't know whether to believe them or laugh at the ridiculousness of someone saying them to her.

It was at that point that James pulled Abby close and kissed her like she'd never been kissed before, seemingly conveying more than words ever could in the simplest and sweetest of kisses. Abby swooned, gazing up into those beautiful eyes of his, her heart bursting with emotion.

"Shit," she thought, recognising the emotions now coursing through her veins as something she hadn't thought she'd ever feel again.

"You hurt me," Abby whispered. "No-one's ever said something that's made me feel so incompetent before, not anyone I actually wanted to believe the best of me..." Abby's voice trailed away, unsure quite were she was going with this.

"Abby," James said, his hand on her cheek, his fingers touching her hairline intimately. What the hell had become of him? James thought to himself, not at all enjoying this transformation into some kind of sappy under-the-thumb type.

"You were a pig!" Abby proclaimed, her voice getting stronger with each word. "And if you think I'm going to cry like a ..."

"I don't want you to cry!" James protested.

129

"Well, good." Abby stated firmly. "Cos I'm not going to. And if you think I'm going to forgive you just because you're using some crap about falling for me."

God she was a firecracker, James thought.

"Woman," he said, loving the fire that exploded in Abby's eyes at his term. "I'm not playing with you, god you're unbelievable. Someone tells you they're falling for you and you have a go at them!" he said incredulously, a smile playing at the corner of his mouth.

"You're just trying to redeem yourself from being an absolutely horrible..." Abby was starting to enjoy herself now, seeing James also taking the lighter side to the conversation she smiled.

"You're a witch!" James whispered under his breath, before kissing Abby again.

"You've got that right!" Abby kissed him right back before whispering in his ear, "And you better be careful or I'll put a spell on you."

"You already have!" James breathed.

Abby raised her eyebrows, "Really?" she asked sarcastically, "We're stooping to that level of corniness?" before she reached out her hand and tickled his stomach playfully.

"So I'm forgiven?" James checked.

"You're forgiven," Abby confirmed. "But ever say anything to me again about my boys..."

James held up his right hand in a scout's salute. "I absolutely, categorically promise that I won't" he agreed, before scooping her up in his arms.

"This feels good," he muttered, happiness flooding through him.

"What?" Abby whispered.

"This." James said, as he breathed in the smell of Abby's hair conditioner and ran his hands down her back, giving her bum a little squeeze.

"Hey!" Abby smacked James's hand away.

"Get a room!" she heard someone shouting at them, and turned to see her boys snickering together behind a wall not so far away.

"Hey!" she shouted, watching them run away, giggling.

James put his arm affectionately around Abby's shoulder and walked in the direction of the hotel's café area. "So, what did you want to tell me?" he asked, his fingers playing with her hair.

"Erm, I can't' remember." Abby wracked her brain, trying to shift all thoughts of happiness over to the side momentarily and find what she was looking for.

"Coffee?" James asked, pulling a chair out for Abby to sit on.

She sat while he walked over to the bar and ordered two coffees, bringing them back with a swing in his step Abby had never seen before. She smiled at him, loving the feeling of being the one who could make someone else so happy. And then she remembered what she had wanted to tell James.

"I've remembered," she announced as James placed the two coffee cups down on the table and sat across from her, their legs meeting in the middle underneath the tiny table.

"Let's have it then," James said smoothly.

"It's about Mrs Cook," Abby warned, testing the water.

"Uh-oh!" James said, leaning in, "Go on then, I promise I won't moan."

"Did you know she had a son?" Abby asked.

James smiled, nodding his head. "I am a policeman you know, a pretty good one at that, even though I do say so myself."

"Oh," Abby couldn't help but feel a little deflated, but cheered herself up simply by rubbing her lower leg against James's. "Well that's it. Eveline and Jane have one of Mrs Cook's old friends up in their apartment. She knew loads about Mrs Cook. Kept talking for ages! I literally went in there when I left you before and just escaped as I bumped into you just now."

"I should probably go and have a chat with her," James said, knowing he should close off this new potential source as quickly as possible.

"Did she say anything specific about the son?" he asked, his police hat now firmly back on.

MURDER IN MENORCA

"Nothing very useful. Just that he was a horrible person, and used to get Mrs Cook to pay all his debts and gambled all his money away." Abby relayed what she had learnt about Mrs Cook's errant son.

"Hmmm, pretty much exactly what we learned." James conceded. "And the reason why I got so riled up when you told me you'd followed him."

Abby looked suitably chastised and agreed to wait for him while he went to have a chat with Miss Cherry.

Settling in with a fresh coffee and her kindle that she fished out from her bag, Abby was surprised when James reappeared a mere 10 minutes later.

"How on earth did you do that?" Abby asked, remembering how long it took Miss Cherry to tell her story the first time round.

"I used the term 'police business' a lot to move things along," James smiled.

"Naughty," said Abby.

CAT PRESTON

CHAPTER NINETEEN

"I've got to get back to the station and check where we are on a few things," James said. "Fancy a wander?"

"Sure," Abby smiled up at him, taking his hand as he reached down to help her up.

Abby started walking next to James, as they got to the main entrance deciding to head to the shops to pick some gifts while she had a spare couple of hours to while away. As she went to cross the road, completely lost in her own thoughts, she felt James's hand grab her arm. She looked at him sharply as he said "Careful!" quickly realising she had been about to step into the road and into the path of an oncoming taxi.

"Oops! Thanks," she said, before her attention was caught by something in the back of the taxi. She squinted, looking closer at the man in the back of the car.

"James!" she shouted, pointing at the back of the cab. James followed Abby's gaze and found himself looking at the back of a man's head through the taxi. The thing that stuck out was the hair, sticking up in one slick shape.

"That's him!" Abby called as she made to move around the car, banging on the back of it.

James ran after the taxi, the driver noticing them both from his rear view mirror and slowing, before coming to a stop as he noticed James's badge, which James was waving in the air.

As the taxi came to a standstill the man in the back seat threw the door open and started running back toward the hotel. James started sprinting after him, leaving Abby watching in horror as Eveline and Jane appeared out of the hotel doors, quickly realising what was going on.

Eveline threw her handbag at the approaching man, whacking him right in the face. Momentarily stunned, the man slowed just enough for James to reach him and wrestle him to the floor.

With the man's hands secured behind his back with James's handcuffs, James looked up appreciatively at the two ladies, thanking them for their support before dialling in the incident to the police station.

While they waited for the police car to turn up to take the man away Abby walked over to James, wanting to check he was okay.

"I'm fine," James confirmed, standing up to greet Abby. He touched her back lightly, reassuringly, wanting to convey in actions what he couldn't say with words.

As the police car approached, James made the man stand and he was escorted away. Abby went over to the hotel entrance where a little crowd was now gathering. Eveline and Jane gave her a little wave.

"Nice move Eveline!" Abby congratulated her friend.

"I'm a fantastic bowler. Hit my target every time!" Eveline grinned proudly.

The crowd started to chatter, humming with excitement. James walked over cautiously, not wanting to get embroiled in a question and answer session with the curious bystanders.

"I'm going to talk to the taxi driver and then head on into the station," he said quietly to Abby.

"Will I see you later?" Abby asked.

"I'll give you a call when I'm on my way back," James confirmed, squeezing Abby's hand lightly.

Abby watched him go, sighing.

MURDER IN MENORCA

CHAPTER TWENTY

"Abby," Jane called out, breaking Abby out of her dreamlike state. "We're heading to Paolo's. Are you coming?"

Abby jogged after them, not wanting to be alone after all the excitement.

As Abby crossed the road to reach Eveline and Jane, who seemed to be sprinting towards the restaurant, she had to stop in her tracks as she almost walked into the path of yet another taxi. 'What on earth is the matter with you?' she reprimanded herself.

The two ladies turned at the sound of the brakes being applied. "Are you okay?" they both shouted in unison.

"I don't know what's the matter with me today! That's twice in less than an hour," Abby explained, annoyed with herself.

An elderly man slowly exited the passenger side of the taxi, looking up with concern at Abby.

"Are you alright young lady?" the man asked.

"George?" Jane called out.

The old man turned, and on seeing Eveline and Jane, waved animatedly. "Hello ladies, is she one of yours?" he asked jokingly.

Eveline came up to George's side. "We need to talk," she said evenly.

George looked from Eveline to Jane, noting the concern on each of their faces.

"What's happened?" he asked, his face etched with his growing concern. "Where's Agnes?"

Abby's ears pinged at Mrs Cook's first name and she looked over at Jane, who shook her head disapprovingly.

As they helped George out of the car, Eveline steered him toward Paolo's restaurant.

"What's going on?" George asked, nervously.

"Let's get us a table first, and then we'll explain everything," Eveline promised.

Over glasses of beer the ladies explained what had happened over the last few days.

"Oh my dear Agnes," George exclaimed, clutching his chest.

"Where have you been anyway?" Jane asked. "We didn't know where you lived, or even your full name to get the police to look for you."

"I fell over on my way home from lunch with Agnes. I've been stuck in the private hospital for a few days. Knocked myself out and bruised my hip." George explained, his face ashen.

It took some convincing to make George understand what had happened, he simply didn't want to believe it.

When they told him about Mr's Cook's son George exclaimed, "Robert? No, that can't be true."

MURDER IN MENORCA

"It is, George. They took him away not even an hour ago," Eveline tried consoling him by patting his hand, but he withdrew it, sinking into his chair with the saddest look on his face.

They all remained quiet for a while, sipping their beer and allowing George the time he needed to process all the unwanted information.

"But how can they think Robert did it?" he finally asked.

"George, I'm so sorry," Abby tried to explain "but it appears that Mrs Cook, Agnes, was poisoned."

"No!" George said flatly. "No, that's not right."

"It is dear," Eveline tried.

"No," George insisted. "No, it isn't." George then buried his head in his hands, not moving for the longest time.

Paolo came over quietly and replenished all the drinks before slipping away. They sat, silently, waiting for George to explain.

Abby's phone beeped with a missed call from James. She texted him straightaway, telling him where she was, and asking him to meet her there. Surely James, with all his interrogation talents, could coax George into revealing whatever it was that he knew.

George raised his head, "I guess I better get down to the police station and get Robert released," he said slowly, looking like he had the weight of the world on his shoulders.

"There's no need," Abby said softly, relief flooding over her as she saw James walking in through the door.

He waved at her and she hurried over to meet him, trying to explain who the man was they were sitting with and what had been said so far.

"Mr…" James held a hand out to the elderly man as he approached the table.

The man rose slowly, shaking James's hand weakly before collapsing back into the chair. "It's Foster," he said, "George Foster."

"And I believe you knew Mrs Cook?" James asked.

"I did indeed," George nodded.

Abby interrupted, asking whether the three of them should move away while the two men talked but George was having none of it, and James didn't seem to mind, glad that the man had some support in the form of Eveline and Jane, who were sitting on either side of him acting like his bodyguards.

"So if you want to just start from wherever you think you should start, and fill me in on anything you feel is pertinent," James advised kindly, glancing at Abby and giving her a tight smile.

"We were childhood sweethearts, Agnes and I, until our parents dragged us apart, thinking we were far too close for our ages. And then over 50 years later we meet again, right here in this restaurant." George started his story, his eyes misting over as he remembered the past.

MURDER IN MENORCA

James made encouraging sounds and moved the conversation on appropriately as George revealed how he and Agnes had realised they were both widowed and lonely, and had agreed to meet in the exact same location at the exact same time every single year.

"For 7 years we have been coming here, keeping to ourselves and sharing two weeks of blissful happiness together, not even telling our children about each other," George explained wistfully.

"When I found out Agnes was unwell, well we talked silly talk, you know, about how it would be nice to die together, and how neither one of us could face losing a loved one again." George wiped a stray tear from the corner of his eye, taking a breath and drinking some of his beer before continuing with his story.

"Then when we found out that I had developed cancer, it just seemed fitting to follow through on what we had talked about. We were both on our way out, why not make it just that little bit more special." He looked from one to another, somehow taking from their reactions whether he should continue or not, but the faces staring back at him told him to go on, and so he did. George revealed how Agnes had procured some arsenic and had created a special brew they were going to drink together.

"But when the cancer went, and Agnes found out, she refused to even talk about our plan. I'm afraid I assumed she'd called the whole thing off, but obviously I was wrong," concluded George, another sob escaping from his heaving chest.

James cleared his throat, knowing this was the moment he should probably say something, but not wanting to cause any more pain to an already broken-hearted man.

"I'm so sorry," James said, "But Robert confessed to spiking his mother's drink with sleeping pills."

"What?" George's head shot up, fire behind his eyes, "Robert did it??" George could barely believe what was being told to him.

"I'm afraid so George." James confirmed. "But…"

Abby looked at James, noticing his discomfort at causing so much stress to someone so frail, and lay her hand on his knee, squeezing it gently. James looked at Abby and gave her a small smile, appreciating the moral support.

"Spit it out man," George stammered, seemingly now that he'd heard what he considered the worst of it he was ready for anything else the policeman threw at him.

"I'm so sorry to inform you that Mrs Cook died of both arsenic poisoning and the sleeping pills."

Everyone stared at James, disbelievingly. "Really?" Abby couldn't help but ask.

"We knew about the arsenic pretty much straightaway as it has some very telling traits, but we discovered the sleeping pills when the lab reports came back yesterday" James revealed.

"Oh George," Jane said, devastated for her friend.

MURDER IN MENORCA

"She went the way we planned," he said, "She just refused to take me with her."

Eveline and Jane exchanged glances, seeming to have a conversation without actually saying any words. Abby watched fascinated, as the two women practically wrapped George in the biggest bear hug, before declaring that they would be taking care of George until he was feeling better.

"I can contact your family if you would like?" James asked.

"They still don't know about Agnes," George admitted. "We never told anyone else. They just used to assume I came out here by myself. Poor Agnes."

James and Abby left George in the care of Eveline and Jane, who were plying him with tea as they left.

"God, how horrible," Abby commented as they walked back to the hotel.

"To be poisoned by your own son for your money." James said, horrified.

"I assume he didn't know that she'd already taken steps to end her own life?" Abby asked.

"That's the irony of it," said James. "If only the little thief had stayed at home he would have had Agnes's entire estate, just what he was after. But his greed got the better of him."

"I just can't understand how someone could do that to their own mother." Abby speculated.

143

"He was desperate I guess," James offered. "But the sad thing is his mother was almost dead by the time he even got to the restaurant."

As they walked back to Abby's room, James revealed that Robert had flown out to Menorca the day after his mother, and had checked into the hotel under a false name, which was why James hadn't been able to track him down.

The whole affair left a bitter taste in Abby's mouth, and when Luke rounded the corner of the hotel and almost bumped into his Mum and James, she grabbed him and hugged him tight, never wanting to let go.

Luke looked horrified of course, panic in his face as he squirmed in his mother's arms. "What happened?" he asked James

"We found the murderer," James explained. "I think you should probably grab Will and take your Mum back to the apartment."

As Abby and Luke walked away to find Will, Luke wrapped an arm around his Mum's shoulder, and James watched them, deep in conversation, loving the obviously solid relationship that they had.

He wanted nothing more than to be the one with his arm around her, but he understood that she just wanted to see her kids, especially after finding out how Mrs Cook had died. And besides, he was sure he'd see her tomorrow, and the next day, and the day after that.

MURDER IN MENORCA

If you enjoyed the first in the Abby Tennant series keep your eyes peeled for the next instalment....

CAT PRESTON

ABOUT THE AUTHOR

Cat Preston has always loved books, but only recently discovered the genre "Cozy Mysteries". Having read most of the Agatha Christie books in her youth she was pretty happy to find a new generation of writers creating light-hearted mysteries and wanted to join in.

Besides having a go at creating her own mysteries, Cat keeps herself busy with her 3 children and rescue dog in a beautiful corner of rural England.

Printed in Great Britain
by Amazon